JEFF LEE

Songs of the Sirens

From the same author

The Speed of Light (2023)
Songs of the Sirens (2025)

Keep looking.

I

ACT ONE

We promised one day we would run away,
but we never did.

1

Standing on the Plank

It has been twenty-four hours since I killed the Captain.

With him dead, my share of the expedition should be about one million dollars.

But none of that matters now. Because if I don't find something clever to say within the next thirty seconds, the crew will push me to the end of this plank. Down into the ocean.

My hands are tied and I can feel the pointy tip of the sword pressing against my back.

There is no land in sight, and earlier today, we spotted a dozen sharks circling the boat. They looked both hungry and bored. And I don't know what's worse.

Think, Michael. Think. What would the Captain say?

Screw it.

"I know where to find the treasure," I shout at them over my shoulder.

Of course, I don't.

2

Two Weeks Before

I needed to get out of the city.

The reasons, I will detail later. What matters for now, is that on that particular rainy afternoon, I made my decision to get out. So I walked up to my manager at the video game studio and gave him my *two hours notice*. A timeline that he rapidly shrunk down to two minutes with the help of security.

The next thing you know, I was being escorted through the turnstile, holding a banker box and my cactus named Joey. They didn't mess around. Too many corporate secrets, I guess.

And I was out.

Free of the crunch culture at last. Breaking away from all the zeros and ones caught in this never-ending open space warfare. Finally breaking free of my golden handcuffs, releasing my stock options into the universe, never to be vested.

That goldfish had made an escape.

I might be pushing thirty, but I feel I can still stretch the fun a little before I settle down. What was the big rush anyway? I could still be a loser later. Open up a car wash or something. I figured living was now or never.

Imagine being old and getting the memo. Adventure called but you were stuck at work.

The reason I chose to pack my bags and move to Tulum in particular for this next chapter of my life, was simply that it seemed conveniently far enough for me to feel something. Of course, without putting myself into harm's way.

After all, people who come to Tulum are looking for adventure—but not that much. They want popcorn in a bag.

Investment bankers with a fresh bonus burning in their pockets. Fashion editors on a sabbatical, looking for that next trend that could make them relevant again to *the culture* back in the city.

Because irrelevance is the first stage of death.

All of them looking for a sweet escape. Tired of trying to convince themselves and everyone around them, that they make a difference in their field. That any of that stuff actually matters.

A whole generation too smart to work.

So here I am. Another gringo coming down to the jungle looking for some *off the grid* experience with a reliable wifi connection. Because as much as everyone might enjoy surprises, we're all still pretty fond of that thing called the aqueduct.

Millions of years ago, the asteroid fell right here to kill the big boys and everything else, carving in an instant, what is now known as the Yucatan Peninsula. A clean slate to build eco-design resorts that sell the same fish tacos you can find in Bushwick. Except that down here, it's a vibe.

As Bill Nye once said, too bad the dinosaurs didn't have a space program.

Of course, since then, we had to go through a couple waves of genocidal conquistadors that we agreed to sweep under the rug of history. All for the sake of economic growth. Look, over here. A temple we salvaged.

Anyway, I came down here because I wanted to feel new again. Get an easy job, make new friends and listen to poncho music. Rekindle with this feeling of excitement I originally had ten years ago when I first moved into the city. Before I had memories attached to every single venue and a different ex-girlfriend crouching in every corner.

Before I could no longer get lost.

And the modern world can be quite frantic.
Remember when we used to look at email once a week on the library computer?

So yeah, Tulum baby.

Of course, I cannot pick a job cleaning hotel rooms and whatnot. For God's sake, I got a software engineering degree from Stanford. That's why I came up with a little scheme which I believe might just work perfectly down here.

3

La Siesta

The manager at Nomad is a lanky dude with a walkie-talkie. I try to follow him as he maneuvers between the different sections of the resort. A six-foot two watchtower that overlooks every detail around here.

I've been staying with them for a week now, but at roughly $600 a night to sleep in their eco-friendly tree house, the only thing that's not sustainable around here is my budget.

One of the first things you need to accomplish if you are planning to travel long term, is to stabilize your burn rate. And that's why it's time to make my move. Time to secure a position on campus.

A small guy with big ideas.

"But I don't understand," says the tall manager. "We already have a full time DJ."

We pause and both look around the DJ booth near the pool area. All I can see is a bunch of empty daybeds facing in the direction of an open laptop pumping dance music to absolutely *no one*. Just mojitos and mosquitoes.

Meanwhile, the lifeguard is staring at his phone. The place is officially dead.

I spread my hands.

"Sir, what I bring you today is a concept," I tell him off the bat. "And I'm not here to conquer the nighttime slot. No."

The manager stops managing for a second and actually listens to me.

"See, most people along the *Strip* have been partying all night, every night. Right now, most of these guests are hungover, tired and looking for a calm lagoon to beach themselves for a couple of hours. Replenish, you know?"

The manager nods to acknowledge.

I spread my hands again.

"Introducing *La Siesta* at Nomad," I reveal, twinkling my jazz fingers. "Every afternoon until sunset, I will perform a playlist of chill and soothing tracks for the bloated whales that will wash up here to enjoy our fresh waters. Only chill music. No bangers."

"No bangers?" he asks, tilting his head.

"No bangers," I promise.

And now I start to lay out my vision to rearrange the beach club and pool area.

"See, we could remodel this section around the pool to provide more shade. And out there, we could set up comfortable daybeds and booths that guests can reserve in advance through the website."

I can feel that he bites. Time to reel him in.

"We then put a banner on the strip to advertise the new concept, share a couple of moodboards on social media and *voila*! We've created the coolest afternoon spot in town. Plus, indeed, a brand-new revenue stream for your resort."

Always close with the bottom line.

The manager reflects for a moment. The walkie-talkie set on mute.

"*La Siesta* at Nomad," he whispers again, his head up in the clouds. He'll probably take credit for the concept later and brag it was his whole idea all along. And honestly, I don't mind. Just give me the goddamn gig.

"Okay, let's do this." He nods. "What do you need?"

"I don't know. Accommodations for sure. A decent bar tab maybe. The usual?" I tell him.

"You got it." The manager snaps his fingers.

We're on a roll here.

He pulls me in the direction of the pool bar. "Hey Tiko! Come meet our new afternoon DJ." He then leans into my ear and asks, "What's your name again?"

"Michael."

"Michael, you're gonna bunk with Tiko, since you guys will operate on the same schedule," instructs the manager. "Tiko will show you the ropes around the resort because I gotta bounce. Lots of guests are coming in today. Welcome to the *Nomad team* Michael."

I had just cheated my way in, right from the start.

Tiko is the daytime bartender. Kind of a short king, to be honest, but totally ripped. Abs, shoulders, and all. As they say, it's the surfboards that carve the bodies around here. Plus, he flexes a giant pearly white smile that commands a generous tip.

Tiko signals me to sneak up behind the bar.

"Here, stash some of *these* for me, would you?" he says, while shoveling half a dozen coffee pods into my cargo shorts.

"Bro, I've only been hired for a minute, and we're already stealing from the resort?" I ask, amused.

"Don't worry about it. We'll need the pods for poker night later with the staff."

"We're gonna be pretty... amped-up," I tell him.

"We use them as tokens to gamble, dumb-dumb. These and cigarettes."

"But I don't smoke," I tell him.

"Good for you then. You'll be safe from deflation. Now let's go, birdie."

And just like that, my new roommate and I are already bonding over some petty crime.

Nomad is an eco-luxury retreat located roughly in the middle of *The Strip.* The new Tulum is basically a long stretch along the ocean with resorts on the water side and restaurants on the other. You'll find that most of the guests booking into these resorts generally have more money than good taste. But Nomad is legit. You can look it up.

What makes it cool and very marketable is the fact that most of their suites are actual tree houses linked together via a set of wooden bridges and weaved bamboo *passerelles.* I'm trying very hard not to say Ewok village here.

The rest of the compound is nestled under a thick canopy that has a life of its own. Above, small monkeys and exotic birds will argue all day while playing Scrabble on iPads they snatched away from unsuspecting guests.

Meanwhile by the pool, I'm looking at a poor guy trying to take a gazillion pictures of his girlfriend for social media. Another vain attempt to say *I exist.* She grabs the phone and looks at her reflection into the pond. None of them good enough apparently.

Dead people on vacation. Just phones and bones.

Tiko pushes open the gate to the *staff village* where a small community of housekeepers, surf instructors, cooks and land-scapers are sharing dorms. Potato heads and nomads just like me who decided to chase the sun for a little while.

There is an open space with a pool table, a beer fridge and a couple of charcoal barbecues. Some long chairs are laid around a kidney shaped pool where some staff members are playing dominoes. Now I get the coffee pods thing.

Two good looking girls are chatting in the shallow stairs. Mid-twenties probably. Pointy sunglasses and all. They both say *what's up* as we walk by. Tiko grabs a mango from a fruit bowl.

"What's your type?" asks Tiko, picking on the fact that I keep staring into the shallow section of the pool.

"Oh me? I don't know. Let's just say that I like my toasts a little *burnt*," I tell him. "A little crazy."

We snake past the barracks, and I wonder where my roommate is bringing me. "No dorm for us?" I ask a little intrigued.

"Oh, little birdie, I'm a senior staff member here, so we get to crash the Cuckoo's Nest," Tiko explains, as he points up to a makeshift tree house perched twenty feet in the air. "It's a steep climb, but you'll see, the view totally rules."

You could call this an upgrade.

"Welcome home, Michael. Gimme your bag." Tiko motions as he prepares to climb up.

Once up there, the view ruled totally indeed, as it overlooks the staff village, the ocean in the distance, and in between, the beach club where Tiko and I will spend most of our afternoons together from now on.

He drops my bag on a small bed, opens the mini fridge and cracks open two cervezas on the side of the armchair I just sat in. The front porch wraps around the Cuckoo's Nest.

"Cheers birdie," Tiko says as the pearling bottles *ting*.

You know what? I don't need much to be comfortable. A bed and pillow. A table corner to put my lenses on in the morning. All the rest, the resort will provide. And from what I understand, the food is even better in the staff village.

The Cuckoo's Nest is perfect and already, our pairs of flip-flops cohabit side by side on the welcome mat. I glanced into the bathroom and caught a view of the waves crashing onshore from the shower window.

Incense burns, and that smell will now permanently be attached to these coordinates.

But as I turn around, something moves on the bed.

My bed.

"Hum, Tiko? There's a rather big spider…"

"Don't startle it!" he whispers, acknowledging the intruder in the nest. "That's a brown recluse." Slowly and carefully, he reaches for the broom next to the door.

The spider gets a whiff of what's cooking and springs behind the bedhead. And now we've lost it forever.

"Oh boy," sighs Tiko.

It's not the spider you see, it's the spider you don't.

We decided to leave her the room. Sitting back on the armchairs on the outside porch, we both stare into the distance for a minute.

"So what happened to your previous roommate?" I ask Tiko. "I noticed the Polaroids tapped on the mini fridge."

"Oh, he died." Tiko shrugs casually. "Killed himself actually. The kid got tired of the bullshit, and one night, decided to use self-checkout."

"Jesus-Christ," I mutter before taking a sip. Then I turn around to inspect the Cuckoo's Nest, looking for any signs of struggle. Blood maybe?

"Don't worry, he did it in the shower," adds Tiko.

I sigh. Another sip.

"Relax! I'm messing with you, birdie!" Tiko laughs slapping the armchair.

"He just got tired of having his heart broken. Girls coming and going."

Exit wounds.

"He went back up north, to wherever he came from. Vacation was over for him," adds Tiko.
"And where do *you* come from?" I ask my new roommate.

He turns to me with a grin, answering earnestly. "That's not important, birdie. What matters is that we're all here *now*."

The breeze is warm, and everything feels right. Up there in the canopy, I believe a toucan just scored twenty points on the game board.

"I'm starving, do you like tacos?" asks Tiko.

Is that a question?

4

Chariot of Fire

"Are you kidding me?" I ask Tiko, looking at the metal basket fitted at the back of his three-wheeler bike. An apparatus with the main function of carrying surfboards and groceries.

"Relax, just jump in the basket, little birdie."

"No helmet?"

"Not unless you wanna share it with the spiders. I left it outside all night," he explains. "Come on now. The only way to cheat death is to live! Am I right?"

So I squeeze into the basket behind Tiko and put my hands on his shoulders. And with one swift push, we join the natural bloodstream that is flowing down the Strip. Mostly bikes and scooters with some occasional taxis dropping off fresh guests.

I have to admit, I kinda enjoy the open cockpit. Sitting in a car would feel stupid right now. You might as well stay home and watch a movie. With confidence, I stand up, spreading my wings like the Rio Jesus.

Tiko is a natural, swerving the bike between the lanes. Everything flows like water. If there is room for us to pass, he just goes for it. Nonchalant yet adorable. Nobody minds anyways, it's a vacation.

"Gotta beat the sunset because at night, I can't see shit!" warns Tiko.

The Strip is electric tonight. And I'm not talking about the hundreds of wires crisscrossing over our heads. No urban planning. It's an aesthetic for sure. Layers of infrastructure locals have scaffolded on top of each other like the computer code I used to lay down every day at the video game studio. Some organized chaos.

It feels good to play outside, and by that, I mean America.

Everywhere, the cool kids are on the move. Going to sunset yoga classes and reiki healing sessions. Making dinner plans to go suckle on hummingbird nectar sold for 18$ a shot.

Everyone converges on the main artery. With nobody to keep track of *who* slept with *who*, and *when*.

I've known Tiko for maybe two hours now, but somehow, I trust him. He seems to be one of those people who always knows their way around. For the first time, I'm choosing to let go. It feels like getting drunk on a train because you know things will run on time. I don't need to steer anything. I just let the breeze kiss my face through my growing beard. I'll shave tomorrow, so everybody says.

We bump into a small traffic jam.

"Is it me, or there's way more people in town this weekend than when I arrived?" I ask Tiko, pulling my arms into the basket right before they get chopped off by a dirt bike zooming by in a wheelie.

"They found something in the ruins," explains Tiko. "Don't you watch the news?"

Who does? I'm in the freaking jungle.

"They've cordon off the whole area north of the Sun Temple to let the archaeologists dig in. And now, a whole flock of amateur sleuths, spiritual nomads and ghost seekers are flying into town with the hopes of catching a glimpse of whatever was discovered."

"And...what is *it* that they found?" I inquire further.

"We don't know yet. It's a black box. The army has the site on lockdown," explains Tiko, avoiding a young couple on a scooter. Cute girl in the back, alternating puffing on a vape and scrolling on her phone.

Something in the ruins, he said. Interesting.

That explains why some luxury resorts are pushing a new narrative. Promising all kinds of spiritual healing experiences in order to bank on the recent esoteric discovery near the temple.

On both sides of the street, banners try to grab our attention and my wallet. Banners for DJ sets, banners for chefs in residence. But lately, it's the shamans who steal the show.

"See that spot on the right?" points Tiko. "Best tacos in town!"

"It's just a donkey cart," I acknowledge, rather amused.

"The smaller the better," Tiko confirms.

"Don't you wanna stop and grab a bite?" I ask.

"Not tonight, birdie. I owe them too much money," he confesses, before speeding up to sneak pass the venue. Undetected. "I will close my tab later this week once we get paid."

Next to the taco spot stands an army of small palm trees, all equals in size with a sign that says *Growth Hackers Nursery.* And next door is a fried chicken joint named *The Plot Chickens.*

I'm glad there are still good copywriters scattered in the wild.

A couple more pedal swings and Tiko slides into a small lot where a bunch of food trucks are parked in a semi-circle around picnic tables. Lanterns dangle from the pergola. The sun and the moon prepare for the change of shift. Cozy spot.

But the moment is quickly ruined by a pickup truck drifting into the food court. I grab on to the edges of the basket for protection. A tattooed arm points at Tiko from the truck window.

"There you are, you little rascal," says the man in the pickup truck.

"Are we okay, Tiko?" I whisper, wondering if this will be my first fight in Tulum. My first fight *ever* in fact.

"Don't worry about it," reassures Tiko. "It's just The Greek."

"You owe me," shouts The Greek from the window.

Jesus, Tiko is all over the place.

"I don't owe you shit," spits back Tiko. "I've returned all your tools in the shed. You can double-check if you want."

"It's not that," says the Greek. "I've bought back your debt from the Taco cart. Plus, I've closed your tab at the Lagoon Bar. They were quite happy. And now, you owe me."

Wow. Jungle derivatives. Looks like the Greek has beaten the mouse to its cheese.

"We'll repay you later this week," pledges Tiko, head down.

"We?" I whisper to him over his shoulder, still clenching to the metal basket.

"Forget about the money. I don't care," says the Greek. "I need you to do a job for me. And your friend can hop along too. Makes more little hands."

The Greek gets out of the truck. A buff looking dude. Not to be messed with, I assume. He grabs the bike and swings it up into the truck bed. Tiko and I climb in and sit on the edge of the box. It's basically a bigger basket.

I'm not sure if this is an upgrade or not, but we're rolling again. The pick-up truck branches off the main road and begins to drive deeper into the jungle.

Seems like adventure has a way of finding you.

"Try to relax, birdie," says Tiko. "I got this. Remember: You're on vacation! Try to pick up the language. I don't know. Maybe start smoking?"

5

A Fish Job

Turns out the Greek is a local fixture who fancies describing himself as an *entrepreneur*. His jungle compound is nestled roughly a mile up north from the Strip. Some dead-end new development along the river that realtors prefer to call *Edgewater*.

The whole setup looks rather humble, yet quite intriguing. A double-wide trailer acts as the main residence, which on top, The Greek floats a Jolly Roger flag.

Here's the curious part.

Scattered around the trailer are half a dozen above-ground pools containing different breeds of exotic fishes. And connected to these pools through a series of plastic pipes are several hydroponic racks on which sprout a variety of fungus and microgreens.

"Are these..."

"Magic mushrooms? Yes," confirms Tiko with a giant smile.

The water flowing between the basins and through the racks is soothing.

"It's a closed loop," explains The Greek. "The fish poop in the water, which we circulate through the bins to feed the plants and grow the mushrooms. We then feed the microgreens back to the fish, and everyone is happy."

"He supplies most of the *shrooms* sold by the shamans in various resorts," says Tiko.

"My growing empire," brags The Greek, spreading his arms wide to showcase his clever enterprise.

It was said of Alexander the Great that the whole world wouldn't suffice to contain his ego. Yet in the end, a coffin did the trick.

The Greek goes on with the tour and brings our attention over the growing fungus. *Fungis?* Whatever.

"Here you have your basic breed called *Golden Teachers*. Mild body buzz. Soft come down. Perfect for music and creativity."

Looks like most of the stuff we took in high school. Easy breezy. Still, sometimes you take too much and the game flips to third person.

The Greek continues, "And over here, these giant stems boasting a phallic shape, they're called *Penis Envy.* And I'm not making this up. Most popular among trip seekers looking for bright colors and hallucinations. A heroic dose of these will send you straight to a meeting with the high council," he warns.

"And you live here alone?" I ask our host, walking on eggshells.

"His girlfriend dumped him because he got too fat!" roasts Tiko. "The man just lost 100 pounds though. So now, he's just ugly."

The Greek slaps Tiko in the back of the head. He's got a point though. You either lose fat or get a tattoo. The man did both.

"Plus, he's balding," adds Tiko, bracing himself for another slap.

"The more the forest recedes, the more civilization advances," replies the Greek, rather humbly.

"And what about the fish?" I ask, bringing back our attention to the farming operation. "Why so many different kinds?"

"These, I sell to the resorts. They display them in their aquariums and ponds. Sounds crazy, but some of these exotics will rack up a little fortune once they reach a decent size," the Greek explains.

Got to admit, I start to admire the guy.

"That's where you guys come in. I got a special order to fill," announces the Greek. "Some fancy new resort wants to assemble a unique display. And as the crown jewel, they want to purchase a Peppermint Angelfish. It's a rare fish and I don't have one in inventory."

One common thing amid entrepreneurs is that they often believe that the next deal will solve all their problems.

"So you need *us* to take a fishing trip in order to capture the beast?" asks Tiko. "And may I ask in *which* part of the ocean should we start looking into?"

"The ocean? We don't have time for that," laughs the Greek. "And besides, do you have a boat?"

Tiko scratches his head.

"There is another tacky resort located on the outskirts where I know for a fact we can find a Peppermint in the tank of the lobby. Some boomers enclave, an all-inclusive. I know because I sold that exact fish to them last year. And now, you guys will steal it back for me."

"Can't you just do it yourself?" I ask innocently.

"The hotel manager and security know me too well down there," explains the Greek. "But Tiko, and especially a fresh gringo face like you my friend, will just blend right in. You do this for me, and we're golden. I'll even throw you a little extra cash for your troubles."

Tiko gets excited. "Tonight we steal fish, so we can eat steak!"

"What if we get caught?" I wonder out loud.

"Relax, this is not a Nigerian scam. It's just a stupid fish on a relocation program," says The Greek.

From what I understand, you don't steal or mess around with the establishments on the Strip. But anything on the outskirts is fair game.

The Greek reaches into his fanny pack and takes out a handful of gel caps. Places three of them in the palm of my hand. "Here. A handful of courage," he says.

"What are *these*?" I ask.

"Just microdoses. Psilocybin powder mixed with ginseng to go easy on the stomach," explains the Greek.

After a quick look at the caps, I throw the pills down the hatch and caution in the wind. I swallow everything. And that's when Tiko and the Greek start laughing.

"These were not *microdoses*, am I right?"

6

The Catch

The first phase of ingesting magic mushrooms is the sneaky one. Thirty minutes might have gone by without you feeling any effects. At least, that's what *you* think. But inside your belly, the magic is on its way. And that's usually when people make the rookie mistake to gobble an extra dose. But no need for that right now, since I detect the buzz creeping around the corner.

I notice circular orbs forming around light sources. Every color is more vivid as the pupils dilate to take it all in. It is scientifically proven that psilocybin mushrooms can improve visual acuity. In terms of range, scope and pattern recognition.

The pick-up truck has dropped us off at the entrance of the resort. It's just like you imagined. Another all-inclusive enclave. A safe place where boomers can fly in and out on the family account.

Some middle aged men will swallow their wedding ring as soon as the wheels hit the tarmac.

It's another souvenir shop in disguise. Using beach bathrooms as an anchor to lure the families in. A gated village where guests can crouch for a week without ever exploring the outside world. Except for maybe risking a dune buggy rental.

Adventure commoditized.

You know, some people travel far and wide just to order the same chicken sandwich.

We walk in by the big door.

The interiors of the lobby have all the staples of the boomers' design aesthetic. Fake marble columns, big fluffy cushions on wicker furniture. Bundles of branches stuck in giant vases for no reason. And of course, eggshell stucco shotgunned on every remaining surface.

We slide past two cooks wearing their all white in a 80 degrees heat while flipping omelets. Everything you should expect from the brochure really.

Tiko has the fishnet rolled up and planted along his leg while he tries his best not to walk like a pirate. I grab the first water pitcher I see from a busboy cart. Removing the ice floating on top to prepare for a fish landing.

The plan is simple. We will pull the fire alarm somewhere there is no surveillance camera. Then amid the confusion of the guests rushing out, Tiko will scoop the wanted specimen from the main tank and drop it into the water pitcher. At least, that's the sequence on paper.

"Look for a red fish with white stripes," said the Greek.

A racing fish. I chuckle alone.

We need to locate that thing real quick because I feel that *phase two* of the mushroom buzz is about to kick in. Which means mild hallucinations, a difficulty to focus and an avalanche of random thoughts.

Did you know for example, that a dolphin is the only mammal able to withhold its breath long enough to kill itself?

Tiko snaps his fingers. "Michael, stay with me!"

The walls are undulating. There are fish tanks in every corner. We're literally surrounded with water. So much so, that the fish might actually think they are the ones *watching us*.

Did you know that a silverback gorilla can bench press 4000 lbs? They tried it.

"Was the ceiling that low?" I wonder. I mean, it looks like it's compressing. Whenever I'm high, I'm having difficulty to perceive buildings as solids. All I see is the colossal weight under tension. A constant struggle not to come crumbling down.

Tiko pulls on my sleeve and whispers. "Michael, look," he says while pointing at a medium tank in the restaurant lobby. "The Greek said the fish would be alone, right?"

"Yes. It's a killer fish," I tell him. "Can't mix this species with others."

Big fish eat little fish. These are the politics of captivity. Some fish might also just kill out of boredom. Hell, what do we know? Once they figure they're not playing in an open world.

"I think that's the one," says Tiko. "Go for the fire alarm. I'll stand guard by the tank."

And he's doing military hand signs.

With the water pitcher secured next to him, I venture deeper into the lair, looking for the right lever to pull.

Meanwhile inside, I'm peaking. I look at my feet. Not sure if I'm wearing flip flops or scuba fins. I'm resurfacing here and there for pockets of air.

There's a fire alarm right outside the ladies room on the second floor that is concealed behind climbing plants. No surveillance cameras in sight. So without skipping a beat, I pull the trigger.

And like an inflatable pool that is punctured, the guests start to leak through the front door. The plan is working. The staff is helps guide the flow down to safety.

A fat man drifts by holding a champagne bottle, probably stoked that he won't have to pay for this meal. You're welcome, baba. That fire alarm will probably be the highlight of his vacation. A brush with danger.

I hug the wall to let several more logs flow downstream until Tiko joins me with the water pitcher.

"It's done," he whispers. Hinting at the fresh catch twirling inside the recipient.

A small fish with yellow stripes.

"Dude, it's the wrong fish!" I whisper yet scream inside. "The Greek said *white* stripes. *White* stripes! For God sake. Now's the time to tell me you're colorblind."

We both look around.

"We have to go back," I tell him, dragging him upstream against the current. Pushing drunk guests aside. I just lost a flipper, but we can't turn around.

Most of the patrons have left the building by now. It's just us, plus a million CCTV cameras watching. But whatever. We'll never set foot in this resort again anyways. Now where is that white striped devil?

Suddenly, I spot Tiko already nipples deep into another tank, trying to scoop the exotic. That fish probably knows what's up by now and is fighting his way out of the net.

"Faster, faster!" I shout, agitating my hand while scouting around for predators.

"Got him! Bring me the pitcher," says Tiko, right before snagging the water pitcher from my hands to drop the fresh catch. Yet he didn't remove the other fish.

"Bro, they can't mix! They will kill each other," I warn him. But it's too late, both fish are now circling around inside the pitcher. Assessing their situation. Like prison on day one.

"Oh, hey there! Excuse me?" shouts a man in the distance. Some hotel staff member coming our way.

With the powers provided by the magic mushrooms, my eyes zoom in on the name tag. It reads *Hotel Manager*. Whoopsie.

Immediately, I take a deep breath, exhale and begin to chug all the water from the pitcher. We didn't come all this way to get busted at the finish line by some glorified school principal, wearing a floral shirt.

"Run, Michael! Through the fire escape," shouts Tiko, dropping the weapon of the crime and sprinting across the kitchen.

If we want no beef, we better go chicken.

My eyes squint and my jaw dislocates to capacity, *anaconda style*, until I've emptied the full content of the pitcher into my stomach. Everybody in, no time to explain. Then I break the pitcher on the floor, sending glittering shards in every direction.

I run past the cash registers and into the bamboo garden where Tiko is waiting for me. We're both laughing like madmen.

Meanwhile in my stomach, I feel a tingle. May the best fish win.

As planned, the Greek is waiting with the pick-up truck at the end of the service road. Engine running. We plunge into the truck bed, and Tiko bangs two times on the cabin. We screech off into the night.

As we escape on the dirt road, Tiko hands me a construction helmet, hoping everyone is safe in there.

With two fingers down my throat, I'm working hard to extract the cargo. And finally, both fish slide down into the helmet squeezed between my legs.

Plop plop, fizz fizz. What a relief it is.

"Side quest completed!" shouts Tiko. "Here. Cleanse yourself with this." He hands me a bottle of rum he managed to snatch from behind the bar of the resort.

I might have quenched half of that bottle in one gulp just to erase the taste of the whole experience in my mouth.

Now *phase three* of a mushroom trip is called *the come down,* where the buzz gently fades away. Putting an end to the simulation and leaving you with the feeling that you've actually learned something.

And I've only known Tiko for ten hours.

7

Discovery in the Ruins

The rooster is particularly pissed off this morning and made sure we all knew about it. I guess sleeping late is not on the menu. But if he doesn't shut up soon, I swear *he* will be.

With one eye open, I scan my surroundings. Long chairs, fruit bowl. This is ground level. I must have fallen asleep around the pool. Thank god I didn't try to climb up in the Cuckoo's Nest last night after we finished polishing off that Rum bottle.

Cold water splashes on my chest. What the hell?

"Wake up, coconut!" shouts Tiko from the nest. He's cranking up a super-soaker. He aims it again and hits me with another water projectile. How old is he?

Meanwhile the manager towers over my lifeless body.

"Oh Michael, there you are," he says, clipping the walkie-talkie to his belt.

Here I am.

"Nice sunglasses, by the way," he adds.

This is my secret. I look good in cheap frames.

"Listen, the marketing team is about to fire the newsletter to promote our new afternoon concept. What should they write down as your *DJ name?*" he asks.

Shit got real pretty quick. I think for a moment.

"*Jungle Michael*," I lay on the spot.

Manager picks up the squawk box "The name is *Jungle Michael*, guys. I repeat, *Jungle Michael*. Same thing for the banners."

The manager looks at me and winks. "You came to us at the right moment. We are fully booked for the whole week," he says. "That discovery in the ruins is a blessing for everyone."

More water splashing.

"Michael, breakfast hut, *now!*" shouts Tiko from the nest right before he jumps on the Tarzan swing that connects the Cuckoo's nest to the pool. I don't think he ever showers.

Near the breakfast bar stands a curious looking man holding hands with other employees. Together they form a circle. He has long hair in a ponytail and wears too many necklaces hanging over an open hemp shirt. Picture Jesus if he had been performing intermittent fasting for sixty days.

The tall manager is part of the circle too. Eyes closed like they're all praying or something.

"What is going on over there?" I ask Tiko on the down low. Pointing at the ritual.

"That, my friend, is Cyrus. Our *shaman in residence* and also official *rainstopper*," Tiko casually explains while reaching for the bagels. "That's what they are doing right now. Pushing back the rain for the launch of *La Siesta* this afternoon. They're working for you, actually."

"Pushing back the rain," I ask, amused. "And how exactly does that work?"

"Don't ask me, birdie. Cyrus works in the cloud."

The shaman heard me chuckle and gives me the eye. And I have no counter-spell nor magic ward to deflect.

"Listen, Michael. I don't know if any of that stuff is true," advances Tiko. "But you'll quickly notice that most of the girls really dig that mystical stuff. So if you want to get laid around here, you better get on the woo-woo train."

The shaman walks our way. "Greetings, stranger," says Cyrus, looking deep into my soul while I clench a brioche. "I sense a disturbance in your aura. You must be nervous about your act coming up this afternoon?"

"I guess," I reply, totally spellbound.

Meanwhile, two members of the National Defense Army, sporting full green uniforms with loaded rifles, are entering the staff village. Pushing aside furniture, looking underneath the tables and all.

Shaking the trees.

"I've heard they've increased security all around the resort," says Tiko. "They've installed a metal detector for guests checking in. Apparently, the Cartels are clashing with the Army up north, near the ruins. They are trying to take over the site. Casualties on both sides."

It was just a matter of time. Yet maybe some treasures are not meant to be found.

Cyrus hasn't blinked for a minute and keeps staring at me. "We don't need violence here Michael, don't we?"

"Give him a break, Cyrus, he's clean as a whistle," says Tiko. "Tell me, *oh enlightened one*. What do you think they've found deep into the ruins? Some ancient artifact, or something."

The shaman pauses for a moment.

"I believe it's a map," he says.

8

Newcomers

The resort staff and the manager finish burying the black wires under the sand, so nobody will trip around the DJ booth. They've placed my installation right in the middle of the beach club area, so I can perform facing in every direction.

I've got my eyes on the ocean on one side, the infinity pool on the other and in between, day beds and bean bags for people to crash. It's cool because Tiko and I can signal to each other across the synthetic lawn spreading all the way to the main bar, where he works his magic.

It's two o'clock and already half of the daybeds are reserved.

My square DJ booth also acts as the VIP section. Another genius idea of mine, allowing a handful of guests to hang out with me on the sofas while I curate the material. Friends of friends. Key people only.

It's not rocket science. I twist a nod here and there, make sure the bpms are lining up and prevent anybody's day from being ruined by any pop song.

The whole venue is intimate, almost confidential. There is a dense bamboo forest that conceals the beach club from the rest of the resort. A lagoon enclave protected from the chaos of the strip.

So far, so good.

Guests get acclimated to the new concept of a slow journey. Some are popping mild psychedelics or MDMA, which are not provided, yet encouraged.

Drugs should be part of a healthy lifestyle. You know, some days I feel more like a wave than a particle.

Speaking of tripping. Cyrus the shaman is busy performing a chain massage with a handful of perfect 10's near the lotus pond. He sends me a wink.

Tiko arrives with my tequila-soda and elbows at the booth for a minute.

Meanwhile on the beach front, a black zodiac slides onto the sand. We're hyped. Two newcomers jump off and begin walking towards us in slow motion. First of them is a tall Adonis man, with the whitest skin I've ever seen. Immediately followed by a slender brunette with perfect beach waves.

My heart immediately sends a memo.

This is ground control to major crush.

"They've been coming and going like this for a couple of days," Tiko briefs me on the newcomers. "Always with that dinghy landing on the beach. And they never venture inland nor beyond the beach club."

"Sea people," I kinda joke.

"They always pay with black credit cards. The heavy ones loaded with crypto," he explains. "They get a couple of drinks, chat with Cyrus for a while and then, drift back into the ocean with the zodiac."

Interesting crowd. The two strangers walk by the booth just long enough for me to notice the brunette has freckles. A dangerous combination. They make a landing a the bar, forcing Tiko to move back to his post.

Who are they?

I'm usually a cool cat, but this time, curiosity is killing me. With the playlist on autopilot, I perch the headphones on the mixer and cross the lawn towards the bar.

The brunette is by herself, chatting with Tiko while the tall translucent man is ordering food at the cafe hut. I casually slide into Tiko's peripheral, hoping he will reel me in.

"Oh, by the way, have you met *Jungle Michael*?" says Tiko as an introduction, right before he turns around to tend to the next guests. Such a smooth operator.

"Hey there, jungle boy. My name is Melody," says the brunette.

Of course, it is.

"So...where do you guys come from?" I ask her, unsure of how to start that fire.

Melody closes one eye and points a finger gun in the direction of the ocean.

"So you are a siren?" I ask.

"The white boat, you goof," she replies laughing and hinting at a long catamaran anchored in the distance. Might be a 60-footer. "This is our home and office."

"What brings you guys here?" I dig deeper.

"Aren't you supposed to program the next track, or something Mr. DJ?" she asks, deflecting.

"Hey, no special requests, lady," I tease.

"We're here for the same reason as everybody else. That thing they found in the ruins. We want a piece of it," Melody explains.

"You guys don't look like most of the spiritual pilgrims we saw this week," I tell her.

"We are treasure hunters," she says.

That's when the tall white man sneaks behind Melody and leans on the bar, flashing a black handgun tucked under his shirt. I gulp.

"Everything *okay* here?" the white man asks with a flattened accent. Norwegian maybe. Viking most definitely.

"He's clean," says Melody, sending the man away to finish his panini.

"I just don't like snakes," the giant grunts, turning away.

"Your boyfriend looks kinda territorial," I advance, still fixated on the handgun that somehow evaded security. But then I remember their zodiac entrance by the beach. Totally makes sense.

"Not my boyfriend," she says. "That's the Albino. He's a former Swedish special ops. Dog sled unit. Now he's in charge of security for our expedition. Some say he escaped from a lab."

She's kinda funny and free. And now I think I'm in love with a tomb raider.

She continues. "Last night the Cartels secured the digging site near the ruins. At least, that's what we heard. And that complicates things a bit. That's why the Albino is a bit tense with everyone today. Better be good or be gone."

Treasure hunters. The army, then the Cartels. What *is it* that they've found up there in the ruins?

"Gotta go chat with your shaman now. Do you surf, Jungle Michael?" she asks.

"Do I *surf*?" I reply, as she empties her paloma.

No time to reply. She paddles away to meet with Cyrus. Meanwhile on the speakers, Moby is playing.

Honey don't leave me, all by myself.

9

The Fountain

The Albino stands still in the corner of the VIP, constantly scanning the area for potential threats.

Cyrus is sitting with Melody, all business and no massages this time. I wear my headphones with the sound off, so I can eavesdrop on their conversation.

"With the Cartels in control of the ruins, you guys don't have a lot of options," lays out Cyrus. "You either have to wait until that thing is on a transport and easier to steal or, you can trigger the army to fight back and do the dirty work for you."

Classic strategy. Piss off both sides and control the argument.

"You like chaos, don't you?" asks Melody to the shaman. He smiles.

"There is a rich place where the river meets the ocean. That's where everything happens," Cyrus replies. Always with the charades, this one.

Unable to play crouching tiger any longer, I program a chill track by *Azure Blue* and join in on the conversation.

"So you're gonna try to steal *that thing*?" I ask Melody, quite bluntly. "Do you also believe it's a map?"

Melody says nothing, and instead, crushes the grapefruit of her second paloma with the tip of her metal straw.

"Are you familiar with the legend of *The Fountain*, Michael?" goes Cyrus.

"Isn't it some pirate myth? About living forever?" I shyly attempt.

"It's a folklore that survived through many generations and was passed down among many cultures. Most of which surprisingly have never even met. Something universal like *The Great Flood* which you will find slight variations throughout their respective scriptures."

Melody jumps in on the storytelling.

"Europeans mostly heard of this story in the form of *The Fountain of Youth*, as depicted in the private journals of explorer Ponce de León. Historians confirmed he accompanied Christopher Columbus on his second voyage to the New World."

"But tales of sacred, restorative waters existed well before the birth of the Spanish conquistador. Alexander the Great for example, was said to have come across a healing 'river of paradise' in the fourth century B.C. And similar legends surfaced in such disparate locations such as the Canary Islands, Japan, Polynesia and England."

One look at Melody and I quickly gather that this is a serious matter for all of them. They both marvel at the idea that this thing might be real. Are we really talking about the pursuit of eternal youth as a *real thing* here?

Cyrus continues, focusing on the Caribbean lore, "For several years, the Spanish explorer and his crew sailed the Caribbean hoping to discover the coveted location of *The Fountain*. A fresh water source with the powers to rejuvenate back to vigor, any sailor who would approach it with a pure heart. Of course that drove them all mad. Most of them willing to die for a chance to live forever."

"Maybe they never found it," adds Melody. "Or maybe they did? And maybe some of these pirates are still walking among us today. Who knows?"

Okay. Now I'm totally locked in.

The Fountain of Youth.

"Michael, the music!" screams Tiko from the bar now that the playback went silent for more than a minute.

I put the needle back on.

"So you're telling me that The Fountain is what your *expedition* is looking for?" I ask Melody, still a bit shell shocked.

"At least that's the main quest," she says. "In the meantime, we still need to find a way to bankroll the rest of the voyage."

Eternal life.

Something most fools were ready to die for.

Suddenly, the Albino rushes into the VIP section and pulls Melody by the arm. "Time to fly, look," he says, hinting subtlety at the two army men who are about to enter the beach club.

"You surf, Michael?" Melody asks, yet again, not waiting for an answer.

10

El Cangrejo

When Tiko pulled on my toes to wake me up before sunrise, he presented me with a coffee and a banana. He was already jolted up. What did he smoke, catnip?

"Grab this," he said. "You'll swallow plenty of water later."

Today was the day. I didn't want to tell Tiko and especially Melody, but this morning would be my first time venturing on a surfboard. How hard could it be anyways? I've seen the movies. If the kids can do it.

So here we are staring at the ocean. The sun is still asleep, with only the white foam detouring the crashing waves.

From what I understand, today is also special for the local kids. Once a year, for those who are coming of age, the boys and girls from the villages nearby must go through this rite of passage. The ceremony consists of paddling together around the cliffs at dawn, until they reach a spot locals call *"La Piscina."*

And we decided to join in. There is safety in numbers.

Melody launches first into the water, followed by Tiko and the school of juniors. If anything goes wrong, at least I might be able to use one of them as a buoy.

Dogs run and bark along the shoreline, trying to keep up with the kids. Do they even know they're in paradise?

It's only once I get water up to my waist that I realize how the ocean is not a force you want to fight with. My feet can no longer hold my position, and suddenly, I'm taking off. Totally at the mercy of the element. Rendered to a stupid stick floating on the surface. And I'm looking for an excuse to turn back.

"Isn't there lots of sharks in these waters?" I ask Melody, who's already sitting on her board and waiting for me.

"Sharks, manta rays, big tunas. You'll meet the whole gang!" she says, quickly turning around to plunge under the first break.

Enter the water, enter the food chain.

I lean on my board and brace for the first wall rolling in my direction. Maybe two or three feet high but backed by the whole force of the ocean behind. Rolling over my head as I nose dive under the foam.

Then another one. And another one. And once I emerge on the other side of the set, I'm finally able to catch a breath.

Coming to the realization that I've barely made any progress. Meanwhile Tiko and the kids are already safe beyond the break.

So I paddle harder and repeat the motions. And I hear Melody chanting my name like a puppy. Laughing candidly.

"I'm so exhausted," I tell her once I've cleared all the hurdles.

"First time surfing, I see," she nags.

"How can you tell?"

"You tied the leash to your wrist, Michael."

And we begin paddling north along the cliffs as the first rays of the sunrise contour the purple clouds on the horizon. The greatest show on earth.

Can't help but notice that those giant cliffs are unforgiving. I don't see how to climb or beach safely anywhere. Get too close and you'll get pounded against the rocks. The crashing sound itself is terrifying.

Tiko is leading the pack. Good pace.

"The kids know where to go," explains Melody. "Once we've cleared the rocky peak, you'll see the tower."

La Piscina, as they say.

Tiko described it to me as a rock formation that detaches off the cliff and advances into the ocean. The only section of the cliff for miles around where it's possible to climb. And on top of the tower is a natural basin carved by years of rainwater accumulating.

That's the rite of passage.

You need to climb up the tower, drink the fresh water on top while looking at the sunrise, then jump back into the ocean.

Once we've finally caught up with the kids, we use our leashes to connect all the surf boards together to float like a giant raft. Some of the kids will stick around while the rest of us need to start swimming towards the cliffs.

And that's when I see it. That's when I see the tower.

"Are you kidding me?" I ask Tiko. "This thing is like forty feet tall.

"Sixty, when the water retreats between sets," he corrects me. "Take a deep breath. Look at what the kids are doing. And be careful, these rocks are volcanic. Some are razor sharp and can rip your foot open if you don't pay attention."

No big deal.

The first kids are going for it. Patiently, they swim beyond the break until comes along a decent set of waves. Then they use this energy to launch themselves forward onto the cliff, where they hope to catch a grip.

"You see." Tiko points. "You don't want to fight the ocean. Let it take you there. It's all about timing."

Some kids are already climbing the rocks along the tower.

"Let's go, Gordito!" screams one of the kids who already made it to the top.

"They're talking to you." Melody laughs.

"What does it mean?" I ask, no Spanish.

"It means you have beautiful eyes."

And so I abandon the safety of the raft to swim defenseless in the direction of the tower. A pale noodle on top of the monster soup.

I'm waiting for the right wave like I'm waiting for the bus. Man, this is crazy. And here we go. The silent force of the wave building up is sucking me into motion. Then I end up riding on top, coming in fast towards the tower, before I finally crash onto the rocks.

My hands and my feet slide a bit, but ultimately, I get a grip. I made it. I've landed on the tower. That's when I hear all of the kids screaming.

"Climb, climb, climb!" they all shout.

What?

And immediately the next set of waves hit me in the back, with the violent foam crashing way up above my head. And as soon as the water retreats, I feel the full force or the tide pulling me away from the cliff like I'm nothing. Swallowing me back into the ocean. My hands are useless and now I'm falling twenty feet below my starting point.

And without mercy, the next wave rolls in, sucking me away, and once again, launching me back onto the rocks. But this time, I don't manage to cling to anything, and my body slides even lower along the cliff.

There is blood in the water. One of my fingers is missing a nail, and the saltwater burns the lacerations along my shin. I'm totally exhausted. Out of breath. And if I don't make it out on the next set, this is the end for me.

And you know what? Maybe it's not so bad after all. I had a good run. If we lived in medieval times, I'd be dead or king by now. There is something warm inside me that feels very comforting. Asking me to let go. I look at the early sunlight gleaming through the surface. Waves rolling on top. Another day will begin, whether with or without me.

I'm not asking for the moon, just for my life.

I've read multiple stories about mountain climbers on the verge of collapsing, out of oxygen at the top of Mount Everest. They all said the same thing. At that very last moment, when you believe it's over, some magical hand will reach out. Some called it "the second climber effect" or something. A supernatural force that nudges you back on your way.

That's exactly what happens to me at that moment.

When the next set of waves rushes towards the cliff, something, somehow pulls me back to the surface and slams me on the rocks. And I swim like I've never swam before. Not on the water. On the rocks. Crawling like a chased animal up in a tree, with total disregard of the sharp volcanic rocks slicing through my skin. The only way is up.

And so I reach the top. Collapsing into the fresh water basin. The kids start slapping onto the water in sign of respect. We have conquered the tower together. We could all at last drink from La Piscina.

I'm bleeding from my hands, my knees and my feet. And that blood is mixing up with pure tears of joy streaming down my face.

Today, I was spared.

Tiko and Melody also made it. They both hug me for a moment. And then I look into her ocean eyes as she leans forward to kiss me on the cheek.

The sun is rising, and I can feel everything.

11

Paradise Lost

The zodiac slides into the beach at around two o'clock like it does every afternoon. This time with three silhouettes on board. The Albino splashes out first, leading the charge. Followed by Melody, my blue crush, and finally, a man I haven't seen around before.

It's hard not to notice the AR-15 rifle strapped on the back of the Albino. Just another chill day at the office, I guess.

Melody swings by the booth while I'm mixing tracks, despite the bandages on my hands. Definitely not a fan of volcanic rock since yesterday.

"You know what the kids of the village are calling you now, right?" she asks, adding chuckles to the injury. "They call you *El Cangrejo*. Because you kept clinging so hard to these rocks."

I've looked it up. It means, *The Crab*.

Yesterday, I almost drowned at the foot of *La Piscina.* Yet by some miracle, I managed to fight to live another day. Standing on top of the tower and looking at the horizon, I was crying, bleeding and feeling overwhelmed with gratitude. But little did I know, the only way out was to make the forty foot jump back into the ocean. Then of course, paddle all the way back around the cliffs. And with my hand injured, Melody had to tug me back to shore. What a man.

Still, I'm glad she chose to come by the booth to say hello, even before her first Paloma. I pinch her cheek with my makeshift claw formed by my fingers taped together.

"Who's your friend?" I ask, looking at the new guy flanked by the Albino while they both pull up the zodiac on the beach.

"That's Captain Brad. The man, the legend himself," she says.

"He looks familiar," I wonder out loud. "Did I see him some-where?"

"Most probably on those Interpol posters at the airport. The man is wanted in seven countries," Melody casually explains.

I blink twice.

"For *what* crime may I ask?" I'm kind of starstruck. I've never met a real outlaw before.

"Two years ago, Captain Brad and his partner at the time, per-formed one of the biggest crypto scams ever. You've probably heard of it. The media labeled it the modern equivalent of *The Grand Train Robbery.*

"And how much money are we talking about here?" I inquire, now obsessed with this new character.

"They pulled the rug on roughly two billion US dollars. Draining all the accounts before disappearing. Totally falling off the map. And now, Captain Brad simply can't go home."

The Albino and the Captain make their way into the booth. The man extends a tanned hand. "I'm Brad," the Captain says, with the confidence of a revolver. He must be in his fifties. And the good part I mean.

What do you say to a billionaire? The richest person I know is my uncle, and he drives a Corolla.

"Melody told me all about your prowess on the cliffs yesterday. You got lucky buddy. Could have turned out much differently. Down here, you never know what the morning brings you. A coffee or a coffin."

He has that low tone southern accent.

"Michael is a software engineer turned jungle DJ," says Melody, as if she's reading from a cue card.

"Software engineer, eh?" repeats the Captain. "Interesting."

There are many guests moving around the booth. Plates

circulating, utensils clanking. We can sense that the Albino is having a hard time assessing potential dangers amid the casuals. He leans to speak into the Captain's ear.

"Sir, you shouldn't be here," he says.

"Relax, I'm talking with my new friend here," pushes back the Captain. "You're not a cop, aren't you?" he asks me.

"Not a cop," I reply. But man, I feel stupid.

Yet the Captain keeps his focus on me. Which makes me feel like a million bucks.

"What type of code were you writing?" the Captain continues. "Before you became... Jungle Michael."

"Video games, mostly. Open worlds."

The Captain laughs. "Open world!" he repeats, spreading his arms to showcase everything around him. "That's why we came down here. Now if I could just get my hands on that Easter egg they've found in the ruins..."

"I'm sorry if this is none of my business," I venture carefully. "But can't you guys just buy *that thing* from the Cartels?" I ask the Captain. "Make a deal with them for the artifact."

Captain Brad smirks. "It's a bit more complicated than that."

He taps on his empty bottle, signaling to the Albino it's time to go get a refill. That would be his third drink within the span of our short conversation. And they both dash towards the bar where Tiko performs a flair routine for some basic girls.

Melody sticks with me though.

"What happened to the Captain's partner? Is he still around?" I question, interested in diving deeper into the expedition's lore.

"No one knows for sure." Melody shrugs. "The Captain might tell you many versions of the same story, depending on how many drinks he has."

All of a sudden, we hear some sort of commotion coming from beyond the bamboo forest.

Gunshots.

Followed with an exchange of fire.

Guests scream. Lots of them flock into the beach club from the resort and run towards us. They probably think they'll be safer on the beach.

"Shit. The Cartels are here," gathers Melody.

More gun shots and assault rifles are being fired in all directions. There are only a handful of army personnel on the premises. Meanwhile, more and more Cartel members emerge from the bamboo forest. The good guys are clearly outnumbered.

The Albino fires back. Cover shots mostly. He and the Captain make a run towards the DJ booth and plunge behind the speakers. The Albino kicks a sofa on its side to provide more cover. Melody does the same.

"What the hell is going on?" I ask everyone. Heads low.

"The Cartels came to party," replies the Captain with that Jack Nicholson grin on his face.

"I can see that! But what do they want?" I ask again. Trying not to panic.

"They want me!" says Captain Brad.

"Dead or alive?" I shout amid the raging gunfire.

"Doesn't seem to matter!" he replies, tucking a silver necklace back under his polo shirt.

From my position, I can see that half of the army soldiers already lie dead around the pool. Lots of blood splattered on the day beds. Cartridges spread around like confetti.

"Hey Al, over here!" screams Cyrus, hiding behind the cement wall of the pool house, pleading to the Albino to do something.

The Albino fires more covering shots with the AR-15 above the turntables, but Cyrus remains frozen and refuses to leave his position.

"Go get him!" orders the Captain. "We need him."

That's when the Albino turns to me and presents me with the handgun. "You know how to use this, right?" he asks, looking left and right.

I hate guns. I don't trust guns. I don't want to touch that thing nor even see it.

"I don't *feel* it," I tell the Albino, pushing back the air between me and the gun.

"The gun doesn't care what you feel," he tells me.

A semi-automatic rifle bullet whistles by, only inches away from my left ear.

"Okay, give me that goddamn thing," I tell him.

Then Melody and the Albino run out of the booth and sprint towards the pool house in hopes of rescuing Cyrus.

The bad guys are closing in, and I can see that the Captain is looking at the zodiac parked on the beach. That's the extraction point, I assume.

On the synthetic turf, Tiko crawls towards the booth holding his coconut machete. When I see a Cartel goon standing on the edge of the pool and aiming a rifle in his direction, I take the shot.

Emptying my whole clip on the intruder.

My first kill.

Somehow I thought it would feel different. But it was just like in the video games. He'll probably respawn somewhere so I better hurry up.

I unplug my laptop from the audio equipment and shove it into my backpack. Saving only the essentials.

As soon as I turn around though, I see the Captain on his back, struggling to control the knife of a Cartel gang banger getting dangerously close to slice his throat. Captain Brad is not gonna make it.

With no bullets left in my magazine, I ditch the gun and pick up the equalizer. And with a violent swing down on the bad guy, I bash his skull into another dimension. I bet he can feel that bass now.

The Captain jumps back on his feet.

"Michael, behind you!" he shouts. But it's too late.

We hear two gunshots.

The first bullet gets lodged into the titanium cover of my laptop in my backpack. Yet, the second bullet goes right into my shoulder.

My legs flinch and I fall into the DJ booth. And now I'm bleeding like crazy. There's no pain or anything, but the visuals are getting blurry.

A moment of inertia.

I guess God finally sat me down. Who would've thought you could die on a sunny day?

Melody and the Albino rush back into the booth.

"Michael...oh my god!" says Melody, now holding my face between her hands. "Stay with me!"

Man, those freckles.

If this is the end, it's beautiful.

12

Ocean Eyes

Every single bump of the zodiac punching through the waves resonates within my injured shoulder. Melody tied a knot around it with her blouse in an attempt to stop the bleeding.

"You need to stay awake, Michael," she says softly.

Bullets still whistle by, but the Cartels are stuck on the shore and pretty soon, we'll be out of their range.

"You saved my life today," says the Captain, looking down on me with his face against the sunlight "No way I'm letting you die out here."

I guess this is all part of my payment plan to the universe.

My face turns to the clouds. I'm drifting in and out of consciousness.

Escaping tides.

It's my second brush with death in less than twenty-four hours, and I have a feeling we're getting way too familiar here.

In the end, what will you remember?

A sunset and a kiss, maybe?

Or that magic day when we were kids. Running and dancing into the crashing waves under the pouring rain. We didn't care at all.

No, we didn't care at all.

Melody is squeezing my hand. "Stay with us, Michael. We'll fix you once we reach the boat. You need to hold on just a little longer."

But man, these freckles are killing me.

The Albino steers the motor at the back of the zodiac. Thank god, Tiko is on board too. Hands full of blood. Probably mine.

A white catamaran appears, finally.

"Here we go," says the Captain standing up with the ropes rolled up in his hand. The dinghy slows down to approach the yacht. I tilt my head a little, and against the sunlight, I can read the letters at the back of the stern.

The Ocean Eyes.

II

ACT TWO

*Why don't we say that just for once,
you and I go ride with the rebels?*

13

Tough Cookie

When I open my eyes, there's a woman tickling my shoulder with a sewing kit. And next to her, a crooked bullet resting in a pool of blood inside a metal pan.

Through the porthole, I see the open ocean.

"Oh, hello there," says the woman patching me up. "I'm Cookie. The expedition medic."

"And a pretty good cook, too," adds the Albino, sitting in the corner of the cabin, with his assault rifle laying on his lap.

"That's right. I can butcher and sew you back up." Cookie laughs. "You're okay with the pain, there?" she asks, as she loops the needle another time.

I wouldn't usually trust a skinny chef nor a fat doctor. But Cookie evens it out.

"I can't feel shit," I reply. "In fact, I feel amazing."

"Yeah. Well, I went pretty strong on the morphine. Didn't take any chances. We're not all built like Kilimanjaro, over here," Cookie jokes.

The Albino smirks. He seems to be the type of man who can tell the time of the day just by looking out the window. He might be white as a ghost, but his gaze is opaque.

"You're lucky you saved the Captain's life," he says.

"Lucky?" I ask, kinda perplexed. I would think it's the other way around? But I stay polite.

"Yeah, otherwise you and your little friend would already be floating face down between here and Tulum by now," says the Albino. Very casual.

"The Captain uses the Marie Kondo technique for people," Cookie adds. "Anyone who makes him unhappy, we throw overboard."

Good to know.

"Where is Tiko by the way? Is he alright?" I ask Cookie while she's clipping off the extra wire.

"He's fine," she says. "You wanna keep the bullet?" she asks, dangling the metal pan.

I grab the bullet and put it in my shirt pocket. Today I killed two people. And I guess it doesn't really count since they were with the bad guys. Plus, they fired first, so screw them.

I turn to the Albino. "And what is *your* body count?" I ask. "With the Swedish army and all?"

"If I tell you, it's gonna be *plus one*," he says, dry as a martini.

Tiko and Captain Brad both enter the cabin. Cookie and the Albino give us the room.

"We'll just go straight to the point, boys," starts the Captain. "We can't linger in these waters much longer."

With the shooting back at Nomad between the Army and the Cartels, and the baddies we left for dead, everyone must be looking for us. We just pissed on a hornet's nest.

"Since you guys saved my life today, I'm gonna give you *the choice*," continues the Captain. "And I will need to know your decision before you exit that room." The Captain twists a gold ring on his finger. "Damn, I feel you guys know way too much already! So don't think too long before I change my mind."

Tiko and I look at each other. On the Captain's arm, I decipher a tattoo that says *Memento Mori.*

Remember you're gonna die.

"And what are our options?" Tiko asks. I guess we're on the

same boat.

"Well. Either we drop you off on the next island with a meal voucher and a pretty postcard," lays the Captain. "Or you can both join my expedition."

The cabin is dark. Mild waves washes up and down the porthole, sticky with the viscosity of a fine wine. Tiko and I reflect for a moment.

"Better warn you though. Once you guys are *in*, there is no turning back," adds the Captain.

Not an easy decision to make. Especially when I got morphine pumped up to the gills.

Tiko pulls out his phone to show me something. It's a video of a bunch of masked cartel members holding a picture of me. A picture they probably pulled up from the resort website. One of the men is sliding a machete under my neck while shouting, "Jungle Michael, you are dead."

I figure I killed an MVP back there.

Tiko looks at me and nods. Then I turn to the Captain.

"Well, I guess we're *in*, Captain."

That was not a tough decision. Adventure is calling.

Maybe you and I can figure out the code? Puzzle pieces deep

down underneath the rubble. Why don't we say that just for once, you and I go ride with the rebels?

14

No Turning Back

On the sundeck of the catamaran, everyone has gathered to listen to the Captain. It's the first time I've left the dark cabin of the main deck, and my eyes still adjust to the open skies. I take refuge under the awning while Tiko lounges in a lavish sofa that faces the open ocean in a semi-circle.

Two trails of white foam get lost behind the twin bows at the back of the yacht, as we glide under a moderate wind. No rotors. The mast must be at least fifty feet, but I haven't walked around the vessel much so far.

This operation reminds me of a documentary I watched about a bunch of hackers who operated from a cold-war era bunker in Germany. They had their own bylaws and code of honor. Working together for a common goal that is bigger than themselves. The Cyberbunker, that's what it was called.

As for us, I have absolutely no idea where we are right now. Nor could I even read a map if you gave me one.

"Before we arrive in La Havana," starts the Captain with an officious tone, "we must come to a vote to agree whether these two young men can join our expedition. All in accordance with our code. All equal votes, all equal shares."

Tiko and I look at each other, kind of amused.

"Yesterday, we already agreed to include Cyrus as our expedition interpreter with the local tribes that we will encounter once we venture into the uncharted islands."

Cyrus, the shaman, looks around the sundeck and nods at the crew in a sign of gratitude.

"Now, Michael here, is a software engineer who can read and write code. A skill set much needed for our next heist. He still sports a white hat, of course, but I'm convinced we can turn him around pretty quick," pitches the Captain with a chuckle.

"What's the next heist," I low key ask Melody, standing arms crossed next to me.

"Stay quiet," she whispers.

"He also saved my life during the shootout at Nomad, and therefore, we shall grant him membership without any questions. All in favor say *aye*," shouts the Captain.

"Aye!" all of the crew members reply at the same time, before turning their attention to Tiko, still slouching into the banquette.

He straightens up.

"Now, what are we gonna do with you?" asks Captain Brad.

"I say we give him the plank!" shouts Cookie in the direction of Tiko, who's now looking at me, hoping I throw him a lifeline.

"What can you do?" the Captain bluntly asks my friend.

"I can sail, and I can fight!" replies Tiko. But the crowd doesn't look that excited. "And I can steal!" he adds. Still, the crew remains unmoved.

I would also add, *short guy, less resources.*

But the the Albino has already unsheathed his machete. Cookie is getting agitated.

"Hold on, hold on, guys," I quickly meddle in, my hands pushing back the air, as if asking everyone to take a beat. "I will vouch for him," I tell them. "Meaning that Tiko and I will account for *one share* and *one vote* of the expedition."

I feel like I'm speaking fluent *Pirate code* already.

The Captain twists the gold ring on his finger. He seems satisfied with this logic. "All in favor say *aye*," he asks the crew again.

"Aye!" the crew repeats.

And that's another bullet we dodged today. The expedition *ordre du jour* continues.

"Before we leave international waters and begin our approach towards Cuba, there is one thing I need you to do, boys. We gotta clean you up."

He's looking at us. Not quite sure what he meant by that.

"All phones, smart watches, laptops. Anything that has a camera or a GPS. It all has to go to the Kraken," instructs the Captain rather firmly.

Tiko looks at his phone. "But...I got my whole life in there," he pleads.

"Exactly," replies the Captain, grabbing the device from his hand.

"Today, you become one of us," Melody says, turning to me. She then grabs my broken laptop with the bullet still lodged on the cover. The hole on top looks like a traveler's sticker. "Today, you become a ghost."

And just like that, both of our phones and the titanium laptop are thrown overboard. With one final glimmering goodbye into the sunlight, they slowly descend into the abyss. Never to be seen again.

With that, the whole crew gathers around us, and together, begin to chant *The Pledge.*

I shall honor the pact
Whether I'm a sailor or a cat
Not a traitor, not a rat
From the snout to the tail
And across the seven seas
I belong to you
And you belong to me

In his journal, the Captain proceeds to enter the following names:

Captain Brad – Navigation and Coding
Tiko – Second Mate
Albino – Muscles
Cookie *– Food and Medicine*
Michael – Coding
Melody – Flight Controls
Cyrus – Interpreter

I look at the sky. The fifty-foot mast of The Ocean Eyes is in a glorious display of its full power, fending the air with a giant sail spread like a wing.

Carrying on its back the GOP of a small country.

Fly like an eagle. Into the future.

15

To Havana

"I was under the impression you guys had infinite money?" I ask Melody sitting to my left. The whole family is assembled for a meal at the long dinner table set in the middle of the upper deck.

Cookie prepared a spicy pork roast along with a giant bowl of Balinese Nasi Goreng that we're passing around the table. An homage to our fellow Indonesian pirates, which in my opinion, were way better looking.

Tiko is poking his meal with the chopsticks. "What is this, catfish bait?" he whispers to me.

"That's kimchi, you idiot," replies Cookie who overheard his comment.

And I ask again, "Why is the expedition planning a raid?"

"The coffers are empty," replies Melody, forwarding the rice bowl to Tiko.

"We are broke, that's what she means," Cookie adds, leaning across the table.

The Captain sits in the patriarch seat at the end of the table, discussing plans with the Albino and Cyrus. I thought they were looking at a map of the area or something, but it's a stupid pamphlet for a music festival.

"There's money all around. You just gotta be quick enough to grab it," says Cookie.

"What happened with the two billion dollars in crypto that the Captain stole with his partner?" I ask Melody.

The girls look at each other for a moment. Cookie raises her eyebrows. "If you get him drunk enough, he might tell you the story," she says, tainted with her usual sarcasm.

The Captain leaves the table to attend to the wheel for a minute, ensuring we are still pointing northeast and on track to reach the port of La Havana in the morning.

Until then, I guess we'll just pass the bottle around.

"You know, it's in La Havana that notorious lady-pirate Mary Read was uncovered. She's been dressing like a man for years in order to jump on different crews," explains Melody.

"If she was the man for the job," says Cookie.

"It's hard to wrap our minds around the amount of loot and fortune some of these expeditions plundered in the golden days of piracy," adds Melody. "Pirate Bartholomew Roberts is believed to have captured over four hundred ships."

Old stories, indeed.

"About that pledge that Tiko and I took today on the bridge: *All equal shares, all equal votes?*" I quiz Melody again. "It's part of your code, right? What does it mean?"

"It means that whoever is left alive at the end of the expedition, they'll split the money," she explains bluntly.

"And *when* does it *end*, exactly?" I ask, kinda confused.

"When we get our hands on the treasure, love," Cookie says. "When we manage to retrieve those billions in crypto that the Captain lost."

Lost?

"All the rest in between is just lunch money, really." Melody adds. "To keep us afloat while we pursue the main quest."

"We were planning on reselling the Tulum artifact on the black market. That's why we came to Nomad," explains Cookie. "We've burn through a hefty amount of resource there for nothing."

"At least you salvaged us!" says Tiko, with his giant white

smile.

"For now, you're just a pebble in my shoe," Cookie shrugs wearily.

And my mind wanders. Two freaking billion dollars. I want to know that story. I *need* to know that story. Yet, I fear the Captain is not drunk enough. So I stand up and propose a toast to accelerate the process.

"Everyone, fill your glass!" I begin, while raising my mug filled with spiced rum. "To *living forever!*" I shout.

And the Captain looks at me across the table. He adds, "Forever *and a day.*"

Of course.

"Forever and a day!" we all shout.

We take a shot, then another one. There's not a single phone in sight.

The Albino and the Captain seem to have come to some sort of an agreement. Satisfied, Captain Brad stabs his knife into the pamphlet on the wooden table and stands up.

"Listen up, everybody!" he starts. "Big Al and I have figured our next raid."

Everyone around the table gets excited. Whistles and howls

over the sound of the metal mugs clinking.

"Five days from now the Bonkers Festival will begin in Nassau. Some preppy music festival for rich kids to fly in and spend a fortune, drinking barbicide cocktails and snort ketamine while the EDM is pumping hard," projects the Captain. "That's exactly where we'll strike my friends!"

More mugs clinking. Big gulps swinging. Blood in the water. They all smelled it.

"Hey, oh. Does it mean more *killing*?" asks Tiko, looking rather troubled. "I mean, I was okay with taking out a couple of baddies. But now trust fund babies?" he asks.

"Relax. It's a *hacking* thing. We've been scheming about pulling off this trick for a while. And now with Bonkers Fest, the occasion has presented itself on a silver platter. Thousands of rich kids will be stuck on the same rock for three days," explains Melody.

"And loaded up to the gills," adds The Captain.

Cookie grins.

"Don't worry, love, we'll just run circles around them," she tells Tiko. "Herd them like sheep and tickle their wallet a little."

<h1 style="text-align:center">16</h1>

The Plane Crash

I brush past Melody as she exits the Captain's quarters. Her hair all mixed up. Does she and the Captain? I don't want to think about it.

Slowly closing the door behind her she says "Careful if you go in there. Captain Brad has been quite flirty with the bottle tonight."

"Just the bottle?" I ask. But she jets off.

Cookie told me earlier that the Captain's mood could be rather *quantic* whenever one decides to step into his chambers. What will you observe this time? Is it *drunk* Captain? *Crazy* Captain? Will it be *easy* Captain? Are we walking on the sunny side of the deck today, Captain Brad?

I decided to enter at my own risk.

The Captain sits behind his desk, with one hand petting a rum bottle while the other balances a brown rabbit that sits in the crook of his arm.

"Michael!" he greets me as I enter the room. "Come sit, have a piece of cake," he says, pouring me a glorious portion of rum into a metal mug. Probably the same calorie count.

The rabbit jumps on the table to come investigate my presence. I reward him with a scratch.

"Don't get too acquainted," warns the Captain, "Cookie's gonna roast him sooner or later."

The rabbit stares at me. So far so good, buddy.

"So what did you want to ask me?"starts the Captain. "You wanna know what happened to the treasure, am I right?"

I nod. The Captain takes a large sip and sets the mug on his wooden desk.

"It was a dark night. The feds had finally surrounded our Virgin Islands compound, and our only way to flee the authorities was to take off using the private airstrip," recounts the Captain.

"We immediately set fire to the computers and to the server room after we managed to load roughly two billion dollars on a crypto memory stick. One single crypto wallet with everything on it! And then we ran to the Cessna."

The Captain dances his fingers over the flame of a candle.

"Tyler was the only one able to pilot the plane, so I strapped in tight next to him in the cockpit and started to pray. It was raining like hell, and we couldn't see shit."

He swings his mug.

"The plane took off in the pitch-black night, relying solely on the instruments to get the hell out of the Virgin Islands in time. And we flew like that below two thousand feet to avoid radar detection for maybe an hour. But it didn't take much longer for us to grow a tail. It was raining and cloudy, but still, we could see some other plane's headlights chasing us not too far behind."

The rabbit listens too.

"Instruments started to go nuts. Altitude, longitude, every-thing messed up. Based on our speed and flight path, I assumed we were pointing southwest and gliding somewhere below The Bahamas. We must've been following the coast because we kept seeing speed boats searchlights trying to trail us for a couple of miles."

"Tyler told me we were running out of fuel. One engine on the left was already throttling and burning oil. '*We only have one parachute!*' he said at that moment, handing me the backpack. '*Save yourself, Brad!*' he had shouted to me right before twisting the handle of the Cessna to slide the door open. Wind and rain were blowing all over, forcing us to scream to understand each other.

'*I will try to land the plane somewhere atop one of those Islands,*' Tyler explained. '*If you make it, come meet me at Hotel Colibri in Havana in one week,*' he instructed. That has always been our rally point in the case we would get separated," explains the Captain.

"And just like that, I jumped off into total darkness. It was a military chute, so I had no control over anything. Ultimately, the parachute got caught into the canopy on some God forsaken inlet. But I was fine and avoided the open waters. It took me five days to trek back to the shoreline and another two days to finally be able to hitch a ride with a raft of smugglers on their way up west to Cuba."

"What happened then?" I ask, on the edge of my seat. The rabbit also stretches an ear.

"Booked a room at Hotel Colibri and waited for what seemed like forever. But, of course Tyler never showed up. And nobody has heard of him ever since."

Poor Captain Brad. That's often how it goes. The first mouse falls into the trap. It's the second mouse that gets the cheese.

17

La Cárcel

On the docks of a little port nestled outside the capital, the Captain is dispatching the orders. No time to watch the sunset, even though the old city and its timeless arbor command a moment of respect. I've always wanted to see the colors of La Havana.

You can tell you've just landed in a different world the minute you spot two men in the marina guarding the gas pumps with machine guns.

"Tiko, you're going to help Cookie bring back the food supplies," Captain Brad begins. "Meanwhile, Michael and Cyrus, you will escort Melody to meet up with our contact in the village. You are in charge of buying the crates of ammo. It's a simple deal. You guys should all be back on board within an hour."

"Roger that," we all confirm.

"Here guys, take this," adds the Captain, throwing us each a red flare gun. "If you ever find yourselves in trouble, just shoot it up and the Albino will rush to your position."

"How about a pager or something?" I ask, amused.

"We're ghosts, remember?" whispers Melody. "No footprints. No signal. Ghosts."

"While you're gone, Al and I will stay here and polish the raft. Ready to take off as soon as everybody's back on board," the Captain concludes.

Even though historically, Cuba has most often refused to extradite criminals seeking refuge on its island, the Captain doesn't take any chances to venture beyond the docks. Always keeping a foot on The Ocean Eyes. From what I understand, the crew comes here once in a while to resupply along the old pirate route.

Pretty sure the locals aren't particularly familiar with this new breed of crypto thieves. Most of the criminals on this rock are still trading spices, eels and rum barrels.

So I buckle the flare gun and motion to Cyrus and Melody that we are ready to dance. Let's get this thing over with.

"Where do we have to meet this contact of yours?" I ask Melody, as we walk our way up to the village.

"We have to go to prison," she simply says, looking forward.

"I beg your pardon?" asks Cyrus, reading my mind.

"Relax. It's just a bar. They call it *La Cárcel*, since it's operating within the walls of an old colonial prison. You'll love it. My contact uses the venue as a business front to sell drugs and ammo from the back dorms. All the while providing a safe haven for drifting sailors."

Good times and honor among thieves. I see.

"Plus, authorities don't hang around much, unless they are looking for a cold drink," she adds. "Most of them are corrupted to the bone, anyway. And they have bigger fish to fry. Trust me. For us, it's the best way I know to secure unmarked ammo at a bulk price."

Sitting in the sun-bleached stairs that climb up to the village, an old man is dangling a beggar's cup. He has a nice tan. Some homeless people are very good looking. It's confusing.

As we enter the village and close in on the prison, I can't help but notice an unusual amount of white shoes hanging from the electric wires or simply gathered in a pile on the sidewalks. You know, that type of cheap flat shoes that the maids wear. All of them were kinda discarded, yet are still in pristine condition.

"This is getting out of hand." Melody laughs, looking at the shoes hanging everywhere. "It was such a good scheme to begin with."

"Yeah, what's up with the shoes?" I finally ask.

"There is a drug dealer nearby that replaces those little humid-ity packets you find inside the shoe boxes with his own product. That way, he can sell drugs on the open street."

"You buy shoes, you get drugs!" says Cyrus.

"You buy drugs, you get shoes!" I add.

"Yeah, the only problem is that most customers will just go straight to party at *La Cárcel* and ditch the shoes at the door," explains Melody. "Anyways. That's not our problem to fix. We are here for the ammo. Let's get inside, shall we?"

That prison thing is way cooler than I thought.

First of all, there is no roof. It must have collapsed at some point, and now, it's an open air bar, surrounded with the original stone walls of the former jail block. A rusty chandelier hangs from a giant tree growing in the middle of the room. People sit on wood barrels around the checkered dance floor. Gambling, dominoes, card games, everything goes. Feels like a brawl could erupt at any moment.

Melody pulls us towards the bar. "What do you drink?" she asks. "They only have rum."

"Shouldn't we signal your contact already?" I ask, looking around quite agitated.

"Get loose, Micheal. You don't want any of these pirates to think you're a *narc*, don't you?" she mocks me.

I place my elbow on the bar and three metal mugs slide in our direction. I take a sip. Yep, it's just rum. We all make the same face.

I gaze up. People can drink here and look at the stars.

Meanwhile, Cyrus scans the branches of the giant tree. Small voodoo dolls made out of rags and brambles hang upside down. Spooky stuff but in line with the pitch deck.

He's obviously geeking out, because out here, it's the real deal. "I feel something dark creeping around," declares Cyrus, who's been pretty chill up to now. "Look over there," he says, pointing to a group of hooded figures gathered in a dark corner.

I'd originally dismissed them as junkies. But these guys are not on drugs.

"They are adept in the arts of black Santeria," Cyrus explains. "Seeking a state of trance by offering their bodies as vessels for the spirits to possess."

"Well, keep an eye on them, would you?" I ask the shaman while turning back to Melody.

"So you and the Captain, eh?" I awkwardly quiz her. After all, things have unraveled quite fast since the shooting. Yet, I haven't had time to forfeit my feelings for surfer girl.

It's obvious that Captain Brad and her are hooking up. I got that the moment I stumbled on Melody exiting his chambers.

"What about it?" she pushes back. Detached.

And I don't know why I torture myself by asking for more details. Feels like I'm trying to move a couch through a door without an angle.

"You guys are...lovers I assume? Plundering together on the seven seas, taking no prisoners and all?" I kinda joke but not really.

"Wouldn't call that love," she shrugs, chugging the rest of her spicy mug. "It was more of a convenient arrangement to begin with. He had the boat, and I was looking for adventure. Brad can't stand being a sitting duck in one place. On that we agree. But somehow, it's getting heavier by the day now. Brad has a drinking problem, I'm sure you've noticed."

"Yeah, not quite the father figure I was hoping for," I confess, taking a sip.

"It rarely is," she says.

"I've heard you guys fight a few times from outside your quarters," I push forward.

She takes a beat and look in the distance.

"Seems like the further away we drift from the treasure, the madder he becomes. Most often he will end up rambling alone in his study about Tyler, his old partner. And, of course, The Fountain."

"Why is he so obsessed with that legend?" I venture.

"The Captain has cancer," she says. "And it's spreading quickly."

I let that sink in. Now it kinda makes sense.

"Can't he seek medical treatment?" I ask.

"He can't. Soon as Captain Brad resurfaces on the grid, he's gonna get arrested. So forget hospitals and all," explains Melody. "So he fantasizes about finding The Fountain."

Now I feel sad for the Captain. Desperately looking for some faraway oasis. And all the roads that lead you there are winding.

"We'll at least locate that treasure soon, right?" I ask Melody.

But no answer.

Sometimes there's just no needle in the haystack.

"Melody?" I ask again.

Before she could say anything, a black hooded character with his face painted like a skeleton is motions to us from across the dance floor. That's our cue to follow.

We tail the skeleton man to another section of the jail block. Looks like an old armory. Piles of cannon balls, powder kegs and swords stacked on racks are scattered around the room.

Still no ceiling. The room is mostly moonlit, except for two torches. The skeleton guide leaves.

Two new characters greet us. This time they wear masks with long crooked noses, similar to those worn by the survivors of the earthquake in Haiti. If my history is right, the tip of the long nose would be filled with spices to counter the omnipresent stench of death following the tragedy. But nobody's dead and rotting here, as far as I know.

"Relax guys," says Melody, reading the question marks on our faces. "It's probably just a pat down before we meet my contact."

"They certainly have a sense of decorum," I tell her, running my hand along the flare gun tucked under my belt just to make sure it's still there.

Without saying a word, the masked figures begin to circle around Melody, blowing some sort of incense powder in the air.

Under their garments, I can see manly arms covered with tattoos. Some are familiar.

Oh no. I lean towards Cyrus.

"Are these cartel tattoos?" I whisper in his ear, while the hooded figures bring the incense in our direction. Cyrus snaps.

"Don't breathe it!" he screams. "It's a trap!"

But it's too late for Melody. She's just standing there, her eyes closed like a sleepwalker. Totally under the spell.

Immediately, I grab the flare gun and shoot the first man into the mask, which instantly catches on fire. Cyrus then kicks him into an empty cell. The man collapses, struggling to extinguish the flames that also take over his robe.

Cyrus turns around, grabs two swords from a rack nearby and throws one in my direction. The second masked man rushes towards us. But we got the upper hand now.

With both swords pointing at him, he grinds to a halt. Slowly we make him back into the cell to finally sit with his acolyte. We lock them up.

That's when Cyrus shoots his flare gun into the sky to alert the boat we're in trouble. Melody hasn't moved yet. She's still standing there, in a state of trance. Like some RPG character unable to fight for two more turns.

Cyrus reaches for the incense flask on the ground.

"Scopolamine, I knew it," he says. "She's gonna be out for a while. We're gonna have to carry her back to the boat."

We both swing her arms around our necks and begin to carry her across the bar. Amid the crowd of dancers, gamblers and ritual adepts, no one seems to notice us crawling around with a passed-out girl.

Halfway across the dance floor, we spot the Albino already looking for us. He was quick.

"Over here!" shouts Cyrus, and immediately, the Albino begins shoveling people out of his way to make a path.

"What happened?" he asks, scooping Melody into his arms.

"It was a trap. Local gangsters or a cartel dispatch, I don't know. She's clearly intoxicated," I debrief quickly.

"They used Scopolamine, aka Colombia's Devil Breath," explains Cyrus. "The most potent drug in the world! With the power to strip anyone of free will just by inhaling a pinch."

"Jesus," I mumble.

"Another minute in there, Michael, and we would have been cooked too," Cyrus says, showing us the drug flask he had just looted in the previous room.

We all run away.

Back on the docks, The Captain sees us coming real fast. With one girl down.

"Tiko, cut the ropes, quick! We're leaving," he orders.

We climb aboard and lay Melody on the sundeck couch. The whole crew gathers around while the Captain maneuvers the catamaran out of the arbor, full throttle on the emergency engines. No one is tailing us, thank god.

Still from now on, I have this feeling we won't be safe anywhere, anymore. Whether it's the Cartels chasing us or the authorities. Someone is always looking for us.

"So you didn't secure the ammo?" asks Cookie, pressing a cold towel on Melody's forehead.

"It was a trap," I tell her. "No ammo."

"We got those cool swords," jokes Cyrus, waving the rusty blades.

Maybe it's all for a reason.

Some nights, I see the stars over the walls of my prison.

18

Behind The Waterfall

In her bed, Melody is slowly getting back to reality. Tiko sits by her side, singing in a hush.

I found a dove in the desert
Just when she thought no one bothered
A little love, a little water
A little spark, the world is brighter

"You scared the hell out of me!" I tell her.

She looks up to me.

"She's gonna be just fine, birdie," reassures Tiko, fluffing the pillow behind her head. He pulls out his new phone to play some soothing music.

We all got issued brand new electronics by the expedition. Clean and untraceable, the Captain told us. Plus, we got a satellite dish pointing to the sky. Our modern-day astrolabe.

Overall, the catamaran is pretty high-tech. Which also means, hello, Japanese toilets.

"I've heard you saved me with your sword, Jungle Michael. A real pirate!" Melody mocks me.

I *did* save her.

Taking a seat next to her bed, I wonder if now's the right time to tell them. I wonder if now is the time that I tell them about *that night* back in the city. I look at the floor.

"I've lost someone recently," I simply say. "She was my girlfriend."

They both stay silent and stare at me. Somehow, people seem to understand when I'm about to say something serious. Something with my face, I guess.

So here we go. They both sit tight, bracing for the story.

"My girlfriend and I worked together at the video game studio. A cowboy game set up in an open world."

"Yeah, we all know that game, birdie," says Tiko. "You've worked on that? That's dope."

"She was a level designer and I was coding. So together we could build things, you know. The perfect team," I explain.

Melody and Tiko both smile. We all meet that special someone once or twice in a lifetime.

A muse.

"So one night at a house party, we had this funny idea to hide something inside the game. A secret place. Somewhere only we know."

"You own Easter egg!" jolts Tiko.

"It's stupid, I know, but that was one thing that got us closer," I explain.

"It's not stupid," says Melody, touching my hand for a second. I keep going.

"Together, we designed a secret hideout. A small cavern located behind a waterfall. To access it, you would have to pull a combination of nearby rocks in a sequence. I mean, no one could figure the combination on their own. Our little place would be safe."

They listen.

"And every week, we would add a little something to the cavern. In the end, we had a cozy fireplace and a cooking pot. A nice table and a few trinkets we had collected from the outside. And whenever we were apart while traveling for work, we would find a moment to visit our secret place. Maybe share a home cooked meal. And sometimes, we would leave little gifts and surprises for each other."

"Cute," says Melody. And not in a harmful way.

"That last week I was working in LA, she texted me to say that she had just added a wooden chest to the cavern. With of course, a combination lock on it."

Their eyes widen.

"I will tell you the code at the party tonight," she had teased me in her text messages.

"What was in the chest?" asks Tiko.

"Hold on, don't rush the story," scolds Melody.

"That was the night of the Halloween party at the office. I was flying back rather late from LAX, so I took a cab straight to the office. Soon as I rebooted my phone on the way there, I started to receive all of these messages..."

I take a moment to swallow. The wound hasn't totally healed yet.

"When I finally made it to the office, the party was over. Ambulances were parked out front, and the whole building was cordoned off with the yellow tape. The staff wouldn't let me in."

"What happened?" gently asks Tiko, now totally invested.

"We were never big into drugs, but once in a while, we knew

how to party. That night, she had told me that she and her girlfriends wanted to do MDMA for optimal Halloween vibes. Unfortunately, the stuff they bought later turned out to be laced with very bad stuff."

"Oh no..." says Melody.

"And just like that, three of the office girls had collapsed within minutes on the dance floor."

"Wait, I've heard about that," remembers Melody, covering her mouth. "It was all over the news. They called them the *Opioid Angels*. It was so sad."

I guess God had a crush on her.

"And just like that, she was gone. That stupid office. That culture. We promised one day we would run away, but we never did."

Melody grabs my hand.

"Sometimes when I feel sad, I'll go to my room and play the game on my phone. Revisiting the cavern. Maybe with naive hopes that something would have changed or moved in there. That somehow, she would have left me a message or something."

The next week we told them goodbye. The leaves were falling in the wind. Black cars only.

Needless to say, it was a very stylish funeral.

"So you still don't know what's inside that chest?" asks Melody.

19

How to Rob a Music Festival

All of the hacking hardware is laid out on the table of the war room, next to the site map of *Bonkers Festival*. The whole crew is assembled to go over the details of the heist scheduled for tomorrow at the crack of dawn.

It's time to see what these hackers are made of. You could say that our expedition has the dynamics of a circus troupe. If you are not doing flips at the front, you are dancing in the back.

The brown bunny—still alive and kicking—hops on the map. I move it out of the way to let the Captain expose his plan. That bunny is so soft and chubby. Petting it calms me down. And since we secured enough food on our stopover in La Havana, our little friend won't have to be roasted for at least another week.

"Did you give it a name yet?" asks Cookie, while passing around baskets of fish & chips to the starving crew.

"It's Mr. Bunny," I tell her.

"Well, don't get too attached, my dear. Farewells tend to be brutal on this expedition," Cookie warns.

The Albino stands next to Captain Brad, peeling an apple with his pocket knife. We're all ready to hear the big plan. This will be Tiko and my official first heist and also our chance to prove to the expedition we deserve our fair share of the spoils. Even though everybody on board seems to view this operation just as a *quick fix* to tackle our cash flow problem.

The real treasure is still way beyond the horizon. That festival loot will be just enough to feed the monster.

"Listen, gang," starts the Captain, "we've been plotting this scheme for a while now, so here is how it's all gonna go down tomorrow. Melody, you have the floor."

Melody picks up a neon bracelet from the hardware pile, so we can all see it.

"The whole *Bonkers Festival* venue is a cashless operation. Organizers opted for speed and efficiency. Therefore, all festival goers were asked in advance to load up money on these RFID bracelets."

"It's standard procedure for big crowds, really nowadays," adds the Captain. "A simple tap of the wrist allows these kids to purchase anything from beers to tacos. Any transaction under $25 doesn't need further authorization from the guests, other than the tap itself on the payment system."

Melody lifts the small square device allowing the concessions to charge for the transactions.

"So here's the beautiful part," explains Melody. "We've mounted these POS devices onto our flock of drones and managed to amplify the signal by ten times."

I like where this is going.

Melody grabs a drone to show us the apparatus. With the payment square mounted right under it.

"Now we're gonna spend the whole day flying the drones over these kids while they're dancing. They will think they're being captured on video or whatever. They'll be raising their arms to the sky, caught up in the moment. And that's when we will tap all of their bracelets."

Wow.

"Hundreds of micro transactions every second," brags the Captain.

"And how much are we tapping them for?" asks Tiko. Which is a very good question.

"Exactly $18 every time," says Cookie. "We've looked at the festival menu online and that's the price of a pizza slice with a soda. These kids won't even notice it on their bills."

Evil geniuses.

"Besides the drones," continues Melody, "Tiko and Cyrus will walk among the crowd wearing these backpacks equipped with the same POS devices concealed in the panels. Your job will be to brush with as many kids as possible for some extra taps."

Mugs start colliding in the air. Everybody cheers. It's gonna be epic.

"Hold on. That's a neat plan, but how do we plan to infiltrate the festival venue?" I ask the Captain. "I mean, *The Ocean Eyes* is not a subtle vessel to just beach up on the island, Normandy style."

"Yeah, we thought about that," says Melody, brushing off wires and chips that were covering the map of the island. The Albino uses his knife to point to a small, secluded bay on the eastern part of the chart.

"There is a shallow area and a beach on this side of the island where VIPs and rich daddies are allowed to anchor their yachts during the festival. They can go back and forth to party on the island, then shuttle back at night to comfortably sleep on their multi-million dollar rafts. We're gonna pitch our tent among them."

"And then what?" Tiko asks, perplexed.

"And then we swim under the cover of the night, right before sunrise," explains the Albino. "All the equipment will be sealed in those black Pelican suitcases that you guys will tug up onto the beach."

He drops the large black waterproof suitcases on the table and demonstrates how the drones and the backpacks will all fit inside three units. Mr. Rabbit gets startled and runs under the table.

"Everybody understand the plan? We go in; we tap the bracelets; and the zodiac will pick us up at the extraction point once we're done," says the Captain.

Tiko and I stare at each other from across the room. Both pretty stoked because adventure is here.

These are the spices we are looking for.

20

Seal Team Margarita

Of course, we drank all night. So needless to say, that this early morning dip is quite refreshing. There is a lot you can accomplish on four Aspirins and a Red bull.

Seal Team Margarita is on the move. And we're all wearing matching frog suits.

My black Pelican case is tied to my foot and thralling behind. Melody and Tiko are leading the pack. Somehow this triggers bad memories from that afternoon trying to reach *La Piscina*. And I don't even have a surfboard this time.

The early morning light which is about to pierce the horizon is soothing. Some say it's the greatest show on earth. Watching the architect's fingers draw up a brand new day. With endless possibilities.

Birds fly over us, kinda blowing our cover. I turn to float on my back like an otter. All the yachts are still sleeping around the cove. One look at our Catamaran anchored and I notice the name in the back has changed. The fresh paint says "Mr. Rabbit."

Very good, Cookie.

The Albino and her stayed on the boat to monitor and coordinate the operation. The drones are also equipped with cameras, so they will be able to dispatch us towards the juiciest pockets of kids while on the island.

The Captain is the first to beach and crawl up the sand with his waterproof suitcase. The rest of the crew follows. We help each other unzip the *froggies*.

Once the drones and the backpacks are all set, we hide the Pelican cases under a pile of giant palm leaves.

"Everybody, check your walkie-talkie," says the Captain. "We're gonna use channel 5."

"Roger that," says Tiko.

Captain Brad unrolls a map of Bonkers Festival. We can hear the kids beginning to wake up in their tents, some even slept on beach chairs, and some others, not at all. Apparently, the infrastructure was botched at the last minute and some of the guests didn't have any accommodations.

"Melody and Micheal, you will stick around Stage 1 while Tiko and Cyrus will blend with the crowd around Stage 2," the

Captain instructs. "Cookie, your hear that on your end?"

"Copy that," she replies over the radio. "As soon as you get the birds in the air, we'll have a visual."

"Good," says the Captain. "I'll be hiking along the bluffs and try to get a vantage point over the organizers' compound. Will fly my drone over there, see what they got behind the curtain."

And we all break up. The tap army is unleashed.

Bonkers Festival sold about thirty thousand tickets for the three days. Most of the kids stay onsite for the whole thing. In total, three main stages juggle the acts and the kids flock between them.

Already, we can spot many festival goers massing towards the food court for breakfast. Large tents and bean bags are providing chill vibes in the central oasis. Other branded zones are also accessible, depending on the status provided by your bracelet color. The setup is beautiful, I have to admit.

All of a sudden, music starts beaming from Stage 1 and hundreds of kids start running to secure a front row in time for the first act. That's our cue to send the bird flying.

On the radio, we hear Cyrus and Tiko calling out to the ship.

"Hey Cookie, we've started tapping kids in the breakfast lounge, are you receiving anything," Cyrus asks.

"The cash is pouring in, boys!" replies Cookie on channel 5. "We're up four thousand bucks so far. Keep tapping!"

Jesus, that's exciting.

Can't imagine how much we can get flying the drone over that crowd. Glad the system works. So simple, yet elegant.

The most dangerous part of the mission though is that they sent Melody and I out here, alone. Her and that flower blouse. The brown hair with the freckles.

She's perfect.

And it took the universe billions of years to generate her.

21

The Kiss

Melody has been flying the drone for hours now, and I'm sticking by her side, playing goalie against the school of drunk kids moving across the site. We're casting a very large net with no threat to the operation so far.

The sun is about to set, and I notice Melody has added at least two dozen new freckles to her collection.

"What's the tally?" asks the Captain over the radio.

It's exciting when we don't really know how much this heist is going to rack up. It's that Schrodinger's paycheck.

"Tally is roughly $124 000 and climbing," answers Cookie back on the boat. "This is good, gang. This is real good."

That's plenty enough to cover our next leg of the expedition. Man, I used to make that in a year. After taxes, of course.

"Sir, we found something," risks Tiko over channel 5. "We found a laptop near the accreditation tent. The computer was left unattended on a table, by the staff restrooms. Maybe it was just for a minute, but we managed to bag the thing! We thought you might wanna take a look at it."

"Very good, gang," says the Captain. "Let's call it a day, shall we? Everybody, let's regroup at the extraction point in 15 minutes. Copy?"

"Roger that!" We all reply in sync, like a barbershop quartet.

"Cookie will swing inside the cove with the zodiac," instructs Captain Brad. "Meanwhile, let's take a look at that laptop, Tiko."

Melody programs the drone to land safely in the cove for extraction. She shuts the control panel and slides it into my backpack. Then, she pulls on my shirt to drag me into the crowd.

"Dance with me, Micheal," she says simply.

"Shouldn't we head back?" I ask.

"You've been staring at me all day, and now you're gonna choke? Come on, jungle boy. Enjoy a song with me."

It is magic hour after all.

"They say people who dance live longer," she tells me.

"Is that scientific?"

"Works for me!"

On the radio, the Captain says he has begun cracking the laptop, and he's already jubilating. "What a bunch of amateurs! It's a flat system. Once I'm inside, I'll have access to everything. Suppliers accounts, bills, everything. We got keys to the kingdom!"

"What about banking?" suggests Cookie, already jumping waves en route with the zodiac.

"Of course. Of course. We'll probably need a moment to hack into the accounts, but it's playable," says the Captain.

Immediately, the Albino jumps on the radio.

"Sir, I don't recommend bringing that laptop on board," he warns the Captain. "I repeat, do not bring back that laptop on board."

"Relax. We're just popping the hood to see what's under," replies the Captain.

"He's getting greedy," whispers Melody into my ear, as our bodies converge naturally.

The music is pumping, and the sun is waving goodbye to the crowd. She's pulling me closer. Hands on my neck.

There is a drone flying overhead, and it's not ours. We both look at it for a second.

"Forget about it," she says. "Nobody is watching the feed. Brad is probably too obsessed cracking this stupid laptop."

And right then and there, she kisses me.

She kisses me, and this time it's for real. And in my heart, a big bang. She then pulls away, and I'm counting freckles like I'm counting stars. Alone in the crowd. The perfect crime. So I thought.

Yet that drone is still hovering right above us.

She kissed me, and now, we have a problem.

22

Hacker News

The Albino passes around a box of premium Cuban cigars. The big ones. We've deployed the water slide, and Tiko is about to launch himself into the blue butt naked, holding on to an empty rum bottle as a flotation device. Cyrus records the stunt on his phone, perched up the central mast. He's drunk too. It's a pirate party, and we just threw the anchor in a shallow sand bank in the middle of nowhere.

After extraction with the zodiac, Captain Brad managed to log into Bonkers Festival main operations bank account via the laptop. He managed to wire five million US dollars to our untraceable account. I know, it's crazy. That before throwing the organizer's laptop into the abyss. The Albino was pretty firm about *not* bringing it back on board.

"We could've gotten more," Captain Brad mumbled on the ride back. But that's all behind us now. We have plenty of coins to keep us afloat for a while.

Captain Brad is now on the upper deck, driving golf balls into the ocean. Melody is there too. We didn't speak again about the kiss, even though that has been the only thing on my mind since yesterday.

"Kids these days," Captain Brad vents. "They have the world at their feet. They're just too lazy to pick it up."

No comment.

He swings, and the ball flies to infinity.

"Wanna try one?" he asks me.

"Aren't you at least a little concerned that one of these golf balls might end up getting lodged into a dolphin's blowhole or something?" I ask him candidly.

"What? Are you with Greenpeace now?" he replies, with his chin up. "They're designed for cruise ships. Made out of fish feed."

Okay, I've looked it up. It's a real thing.

Cookie is on the sundeck, wearing thick sunglasses, and her hoodie zipped all the way up. At first, I thought she was knitting, but she's just untangling the chord of her headphones.

"You look like the Unabomber," I tell her.

"Thank you," she replies.

"How can the Captain drink all day and still be sharp in the morning?" I ask her.

She puffs on her cigar, exhales.

"It's called Vyvanse, 30mg, slow release," she blurts out, eyes stuck on her tablet.

She has been scanning the media all morning. Yesterday's heist is all over the news, indeed, and she's been chanting the headlines as they come out.

"'Ocean raiders steal 5.5M from a Bahamas music festival,' that's *The New York Times*, people!" she shouts.

Everybody cheers.

The Festival's security company realized they were being scammed a little too late. By that point, we'd already glided a hundred miles east, totally disappeared somewhere into the Bermuda triangle.

"Anything on *Hacker News*?" asks Captain Brad. From what I understand, *Hacker News* is the *Vanity Fair* of the trade. For both white and black hats alike.

"Hum, nothing yet," Cookie says, refreshing the browser on her phone. "Oh wait, this just in!"

Everybody gathers around the golf driving mat as Cookie begins to read the full story.

"A merry bunch of hackers took on Bonkers Festival this weekend, plundering millions of dollars from the payment system as well as getting into the operations treasure chest," she begins.

Captain Brad gives a big swing to another golf ball we'll never see again. Melody pops a bottle of champagne in the same direction.

"Rumor has it that the plundering operation was spearheaded by infamous hacker Brad_winn3r and his oceanic crew. Some attendees recount seeing a catamaran labeled Mr. Rabbit, taking off rather quickly into the horizon on Sunday night."

"Mr. Rabbit!" screams Tiko, presenting the poor bunny to the crowd and lifting it up over our heads, Lion King style. Cookie continues the reading.

"This fresh influx of cash must feel very good to the hacker and his crew since, let's all remember, Brad_winn3r was himself betrayed by his partner last year after pulling off the biggest crypto scam of all time."

"Screw that," mumbles the Captain, giving another impulsive swing, this time sending off the golf ball near Tahiti.

"Hey, we did good, people," wraps up Cookie, throwing her phone away on her towel. "Let's pour a round of this Patron bottle I was saving for a special occasion." She climbs down below deck and into the kitchen.

Meanwhile, I pull Melody aside.

"What happened to his partner, Tyler? Did he die or something?" I ask her.

"No one knows. Except I feel that's what the feds want us to believe. He's a ghost now, haunting the Captain's mind whenever he plays with the bottle."

"You think Tyler works for the FBI?" I ask her.

"Tyler was a very smart man, from what I understand. If you're gonna feed the feds, you make sure the books are well cooked."

Interesting. Tyler the ghost and his forbidden treasure.

There are stories we keep telling ourselves. Like driving golf balls far where you know you won't be able to retrieve them.

The Captain motions for the crew to gather around. "Listen up, everyone. Given the circumstances, we will need to disappear for a while. That Festival appearance must have moved my file back on top of the pile, and half of the Bahamas police force must be looking for us at this very moment."

No cheers this time, the crew is kinda sobering up.

"The time is perfect for us to resume our search for the lost plane and my treasure. It's time to set sail for that remote island chain we haven't explored yet," explains the Captain.

The crew gets excited.

"It's time to set sail for Parrot Island."

23

Fireside Chat

"Do you want to have kids?" Melody asks in the direction of the Albino and Cookie. We all sit around the fire alcove on the back deck. The night is crisp, and we share blankets like it's summer camp.

"Kids? Eventually," Al shrugs.

"Being on this expedition, this adventure, it makes everything in the future seem so... abstract," Cookie adds.

She's right. It's hard to see beyond the quest line.

The night sky is full of stars, rendering our ship and problems so small under the scope of the universe.

"But if everything is on the table, I'd like to have a girl, and then a boy, then another girl," says Cookie. "You gotta sandwich this little troublemaker in the middle."

The Albino smiles while staring into the fire. These two are a great match. Everyone can see that.

"I had older sisters," Tiko says. "You know, it's funny. I was born on a Saturday night, screwing everybody's plans. Growing up, I always felt I needed to make up for it."

We laugh.

"Plus I hate having to compete with children for attention," Tiko adds.

My turn to share.

"Me? My plan is to reproduce like a salmon. You know? At the very end of my life," I tell them. "One last big trip, and then I'm out. Buckling the loop."

They laugh again.

The Captain joins us around the fire alcove. He slides under the blanket right next to Melody and oozes his way into our perfect moment. She looks at me for a microsecond.

I can see the stars, but I can't touch them.

The Albino stares at me. What's up, pal? Are you gonna drop the bomb or not? I feel I need to change the subject. Get out from under the Eye of Sauron.

The Captain shells pistachios that he also uses as projectiles on Tiko. I've heard that when the Captain finds something he likes, he eats it everyday - until he doesn't. Then shifts his interest towards something else. And suddenly you notice it's cold once the sun is gone.

"How big is that *thing* we are looking for?" I ask the Captain.

"The crypto wallet?" he replies. "Without its waterproof casing, you are looking at a device the size of a small hard drive. Not much bigger."

"Our best hope is to locate the plane first," the Albino adds.

"I've heard a similar story coming from the UK," Tiko says. "A guy's wife threw his crypto wallet in the trash by accident, which ultimately ended up buried deep in a landfill. As years went by and the value of the cryptocurrency increased, the man finally decided to raise money in order to buy up the landfill."

"Did he find it? The money?" Melody asks.

"He and his army of excavators have been combing the site ever since. Apparently, that thing is worth billions in today's dollars," Tiko explains.

Crazy story.

We've been sailing south for a couple of days now, deeper into the Bermuda Triangle. Except for the moon and the stars, it's a black radius.

"Tell me, Captain, where exactly are we heading?" I inquire. "There are thousands of islands in the Caribbean, most of them uncharted. What makes you believe so much in this Parrot Island?"

The Captain takes a big swig from his mug and puts the pistachio bowl on Melody's lap to resettle in his seat.

"That night of the raid, we were flying in a straight line from our compound in The British Islands with hopes of reaching La Havana. According to my basic calculations, if the Cessna's tank was not full, Tyler must have run out of fuel somewhere over the Antilles."

He stands up, heads towards the cabin and comes back seconds later with a map of the Caribbean.

"See this area? There is a remote island chain that stretches for miles. And at the tip of the chain, there's a larger land mass. That's Parrot Island."

We all look closely at the map.

"Knowing Tyler, he probably crashed landed the plane there on purpose. First, because it is known to be empty, but also because it was probably his last chance to hit land before being forced to crash in the open sea."

"It's been almost a year—that plane must have disappeared by now," Melody worries. "The jungle gives, and the jungle takes."

"How big is that island?" Tiko asks.

"We're talking the size of Manhattan, maybe a bit more," the Albino estimates. "We'll land there in two days."

The Captain stands up and empties his drink. "Going to bed. Good night, crew." And he disappears down the hall towards his quarters.

The Albino mimics Brad's departure, except that he takes a short moment to look at Melody and me. Then, he circles behind me, puts a hand on my shoulder, and moves closer to my ear.

"I saw you with the drone," he says before leaving.

24

A Strange New Land

Seen from the boat, Parrot Island is built like a cake. With clear cut layers getting thicker as it builds towards the center. The outer ring is made of pristine sand beaches, which then morphs into a layer of jungle, thick and rising up like a wall. And beyond the canopy, further in the distance, there are fluffy mountains. I've walked Manhattan up and down many times, and Parrot island is definitely bigger than the five boroughs stitched together. We can't even see to the other side.

The Captain managed to beach us at the mouth of a small creek pouring fresh water into the ocean. On the map, we find ourselves at the southern point of the island. A calm blue lagoon. That's where we drag up the catamaran onto the sand.

Captain Brad dispatches the chores. "First order of business, Tiko and Cookie, you guys will be on team *water*. So follow that river upstream, see where it leads. Most importantly, you guys go figure out if it's safe to drink. I don't like my tea tasting like beaver piss."

"Pretty sure there are no beavers in the Antilles," I snark, trying to be smart.

"Oh, there are. They just wear small Bermudas," he says, looking over his sunglasses. "Meanwhile, Melody, Cyrus, Michael and I will cut through that first layer of the jungle. See if there is some opening in the canopy that we can exploit to launch the drones."

The shaman and I look at each other. Easy peachy.

"Big Al! While we're gone, I want you to perform a full assessment of The Ocean Eyes. We've hit some pretty rough patches coming downwind. Make sure we're still mint."

"Roger that," we all reply. And the whole crew gets moving to their tasks.

Armed with the rusty swords, the Captain and I begin to hatch a path into the first layer of foliage. Not so long after venturing past the first line of palm trees, we find ourselves in rather deep obscurity.

That forest is thick and wild. That's what it looks like when you cancel the landscaper. The Captain lights up a cigarette. We gain like ten lumens.

"What are we looking for exactly," Cyrus asks.

"Broken trees, pieces of fuselage, debris. Anything that looks out of place. We will survey the whole area with the drones once we've established the basics. Melody, battery-wise, we're all charged up?"

"Yup," she says, brushing away a giant wasp from her arm. "The birds are ready to fly."

Another giant wasp buzzes around Cyrus. He swings the ponytail. I'm pretty sure that 90% of the stuff on this island wants to kill us.

"For now, I just wanna see what kind of a haystack we are dealing with here," the Captain continues.

Captain Brad is sharp today. But hey, it's not even lunchtime yet.

"If my calculations are correct, Tyler was flying in that direction," the Captain motions. Tracing a straight line from the beach where we landed, and towards the small mountain ridge.

We look at the razor-sharp ridge in the distance.

All of a sudden, we hear a bunch of eerie screams coming from the beach. It sounds like Cookie and Tiko. Immediately we turn and rush to find out what the hell is going on.

Roughly two hundred yards away down on the beach, Tiko and Cookie run full clip towards the catamaran.

"Back on the boat, back on the boat!" they both shout the moment they see us.

"What the hell" Melody whispers.

"Oh, they met the locals!" Cyrus replies.

Without skipping a beat, Cyrus, the Captain and Melody also sprint back towards The Ocean Eyes while I'm closing the queue.

And without a chance of being introduced politely, a flock of men sporting bows and arrows emerges from the jungle, pointing their weapons at our friends. All very *cartoonish*.

Well, so I thought, until a six-foot arrow whistles by our heads and gets lodged into the hull of our ship, right between the Captain and me.

"My ship, you dingbats!" Captain Brad screams.

Update: 95% of the stuff on this island wants to kill us.

We jump on board The Ocean Eyes to take cover from the next volley of arrows coming in fast.

"Grab the guns," commands the Captain. "Grab the guns!"

"But sir, we don't have any ammo!" I tell him.

"We can at least point our cannons at them," Tiko says. "I'm pretty sure they've seen guns before."

We all grab a rifle. This is stupid. These archers will quickly catch on to our petty deception. We're all dead the second they realize there's no bullets in these guns. But I guess that's all we got. This and two rusty swords.

"Albino! Where the hell are you?" the Captain shouts down the hatch. Yet no sign of our strong man.

Down on the beach, half a dozen archers are now pointing their longbows at the boat. We all take position on the deck, pointing back our cinema weapons.

Melody emerges from below deck. She lets go of Mr. Rabbit, who amid the confusion, dashes straight for the forest. Probably best for him to skip dinner.

That's when Tiko gets an arrow.

Straight into his shoulder. And that scream he makes, it's maybe two octaves higher than what I thought was humanly possible.

"Oh my god!" he keeps saying, finally collapsing against the central mast.

The archers are firing more arrows onto the deck. They're shouting something from the beach. That's when I remember why the crew recruited Cyrus in the first place.

"What are they saying, Cyrus?" I ask our shaman and interpreter. "What the heck are they saying?"

"*Intruders*," he says, looking forward.

"Yeah, that I figured!" the Captain shouts from his position.

Another arrow sticks onto the mast.

I crawl towards Tiko, who's got his hand clenched around the wooden tail of the arrow. Lots of blood dripping on his shirt.

"Leave it there," I tell him. "Cookie will fix you up pretty soon. Just lay low for now."

"Micheal..." Tiko whispers. "I can't die now. I didn't pack for hell..."

"Shut up, Tiko! Shut the hell up! I'm not letting you die out here. This I promise you," I tell my friend, before crawling back into my position behind the rolled-up sail.

More arrows fly by. This time hitting the sofa and the minibar behind the fire alcove. This is getting personal for the Captain.

He jumps up from his position. Ready to give them hell with his imaginary bullets. That's when the Albino finally pops out of the hatch and comes to the rescue, jumping onto the sand in front of the boat, and double wielding the rusty swords.

We hear a sudden gasp coming from the archers. They all take a step back. Hypnotized. I slowly stand up to get a better look.

By some sort of miracle or sheer intimidation, all of the archers point their weapons away from the ship. And slowly one by one, they take a knee to finally rest their bow onto the sand. All signaling they are super chill, after all.

"By Saint-Jude! What the heck is going on?" wonders the Captain, kind of amused and thanking the patron saint of the last resort. We all turn to the Shaman bewildered.

"It's beautiful," he says, unable to take his eyes off the surrendering enemy. We all marvel at the scene.

"They worship him," Cyrus adds. "They worship the Albino."

25

The Banquet

"Explain to me again what is that concoction I'm about to drink?" I ask Cyrus sitting next to me at the banquet table. I stare down into a chopped-up bamboo piece in which the locals poured a yellow mixture. It kinda has the smell of airplane's cleaning product.

"It's called *Toddy*," the Shaman says. "Fermented palm sap wine. That's what it is."

The Captain grunts. Resorts to gobbling it.

"It's gonna tear you up! I tell you that," he says before sending a "*cheers*" in my direction. He and Melody sit a couple of seats down the long table parked in front of the bonfire.

The archers turned friendly the minute they laid eyes on the Albino this morning. And now, our strong man is sitting on a bamboo throne, with flowers behind his ears. Kids are washing his feet; others put paint on his face.

"What am I supposed to do now?" he calls out to Cyrus, puzzled, yet trying not to trouble the festivities.

The women play music. There's definitely something spicy roasting. I'm so hungry.

"Just smile and nod, my friend. Smile and nod!" the Captain replies, lifting his bamboo cup towards the Albino. He takes a big gulp of the vile palm wine. Definitely an acquired taste I need to work on.

"I was not aware there was *Albinism worship* in the Caribbean," Cyrus begins, trying to piece together how we managed to escape being turned into *soupe du jour*. He scratches his head. "It's usually an African thing."

"Well, lots of cultures converged through these islands during the Transatlantic slave trade years. Some were lucky and managed to escape. That could explain the culture spreading around here," Melody attempts. "What's the story Cyrus?"

Our good Shaman takes a swig of the Toddy. Clears out his throat.

"There are superstitions in some parts of Africa that albino body parts have the power to bring down wealth, wisdom and sexual conquests. Simply put," Cyrus explains.

"Body parts?" I squint.

"You hear that Al?" shouts the Captain. "They're gonna cut

you down and turn you into lucky charms. Magic key chains!"

He doesn't hear us.

"It's strange, I haven't seen a single parrot since we set foot on this island," Melody remarks.

"They probably ate them all," I shrug off.

Cyrus jumps in. "No, it's because apparently at night, you can hear things. Distant voices."

Voices?

"I'm already drunk," Tiko confesses, as he's pushing his bamboo cup away on the table.

"It's the morphine talking," Cookie says, whom an hour ago painfully removed the arrow from Tiko's shoulder. And now, my little buddy is surfing on his opioid privilege.

"We have morphine?" asks the Captain, a devilish glare into his eye.

"Hey Brad, you stay away from my stash, would you?" warns Cookie. She's pointing a silex stone knife in his direction. "Unless you let me stab you. In that case, I'll write you a nice script."

The Captain turns to Cyrus, who's been a valuable interpreter so far. "Ask them about my plane, would you? Ask them if they've seen a big metal bird."

Cyrus nods.

Meanwhile around the bonfire, kids perform some kind of a reenactment in the form of a play. One of them wears giant palm leaves strapped to his arms, which form giant wings. Two other kids with tail feathers hold him at the hips, forming a chain.

"There is your plane, sir," Cyrus points out.

The makeshift plane circles the fire, being chased by some other kids with their faces painted like thunder. They make noises, mimicking lightning strikes. Everybody watches. Then thunder starts hitting the plane. They make big sounds. And finally, the wings get clipped and thrown into the fire.

"And here's your plane crash," adds Melody.

"We're definitely on the right island!" the Captain jolt up. "These kids know where my plane is!"

Cyrus being a good adviser, lays a hand on the Captain's arm. "Pace yourself, Captain. In due time. Let's not disrespect whatever rite is going on here."

The women begin to bring food to the table.

One of them rolls out a banana leaf in front of us. On top of which, they present a full spit roasted animal. Head, eyes and all. We gasp.

"Is that…" Melody asks.

"Looks like Mr. Rabbit," Cookie confirms, wearing a penitent frown.

We all take a giant swig of our Toddy cups in sign of respect for our fallen friend. He had a good run. Life is made of hops and down.

"Guys, I feel kinda dizzy," Melody sighs. She also pushes away her bamboo cup on the table. "Kinda soupy," she adds, looking at her hands, trying to figure out what is going on.

"Me too. I'm super sleepy," Cyrus adds.

And before I can realize what's happening, my head starts spinning. And then the lights go out.

26

The Snake Pit

We've been separated in two giant bamboo cages. Boys on one side and girls on the other. And between those cages, a dirt circle pit. Dug rather deeply because I can't see what lies at the bottom.

My head is still hazy. Last night's events are still unclear.

"Michael, are you okay?" Melody attempts from across the hole. She and Cookie wave their arms across the bamboo bars. Caged just like us.

We wave back. Yet, no sign of the Albino.

We were drugged last night, that's for sure. The stupid mixture. The heavy smoke. The tribe got us right where it wanted.

They stripped us of all of our clothes, except for the underwear. What's next? Will the women brush our skin with a nice glaze while the men prep the fire? Are we on the secret menu?

"Hang in there, boys," says Captain Brad, trying to console Tiko who's been shivering all morning in one corner of our predicament. The morphine has worn off and that shoulder wound exposed to the salty breeze must be killing him right now.

We've tried to monkey with the bamboo bars for a while, but the build is solid. The vines are too tight. Below my knees, something touches my bare feet.

"Mr. Rabbit?"

There he is! The hare that was spared! I can't believe this. Mr. Rabbit lick my toes through the cage bars. He must be hungry.

"Bring us a sharp knife, bunny, would you?" asks the Captain. We all laugh for a second. As if he could. But the poor thing just stares at us. He must think he's on the wrong side of the fence. Everything is relative.

Suddenly, he sprints out of frame, startled by a train of women approaching the pit while holding wicker baskets over their heads. The first woman approaches the trench, opens the lid of the basket and pours down a dozen live snakes into the pit.

The other women do the same. Lots of twisting and hissing comes from the pit. A million headphone cords to untangle.

"Oh. My. God," Melody gasps from the other cage.

More snakes are dumped into the pit. They look pissed. One

manages to escape the basket and zigzags between the cages.

"Nope. Nope. Nope. Nope. Nope," Cookie says. "That's a lot of danger noodles."

There must be at least two hundred snakes down that hole by now. The Captain kicks Cyrus, still passed out in the corner of the cage.

"Cyrus, wake up!" whispers the Captain. "Turn on the channel, it's time for your animal program."

In ten seconds, the Shaman takes it all in. The cages, the pit, the snakes, and the fact he's not wearing any clothes. He takes a good look at the escaping snake.

"Hissing adders AKA eastern hognose snakes," the Shaman concludes, as another snake manages to escape and slithers by our side. "Non-venomous, yet not recommended for baby showers."

Tiko moans, holding his knees in a tight ball.

"Cyrus, there must be a way to barter our way out of this?" quizzes the Captain. "We have a lot of stuff on the boat they could use. Decent booze to start with. Also mirrors. They could use one."

"Well, the rest of the tribe is probably slicing up the yacht into small cubes as we speak," I tell the Captain. We don't have much leverage here.

That's when they bring around the Albino.

Our strong man is tied up hands and feet to a log like a hunted wildebeest. There needs to be four of them just to carry our guy. He's awake, but still, you can tell the man is confused.

"Are they gonna make us watch?" Tiko wonders. He's now up and slouching against the cage. We kinda catch up to what is about to happen.

With a huge stone knife, the tribesmen cut the Albino loose. And with one Spartan kick, send him down into the snake pit. And I know I've referred to the Albino many times as being a man of a few words, but this time, we hear him go through the whole alphabet.

That must feel horrible.

And even when by some feat of athleticism, the Albino manages to pull himself towards the outer rim of the pit, the women surrounding the hole slam his fingers with bamboo sticks and poke him on the head until he forfeits. Only to fall back into the snake abyss.

"Now what about us?" I ask the others.

Cyrus hints at the kids gathering in the bushes, some thirty yards away from the cages. They have their little bows and arrows ready. It's almost cute.

"Looks like we're gonna have our chance," points out Cyrus,

with a bit of hope.

The kids make hand signs, pointing at each of us as if they were trying to divide the herd between themselves. A wolf pack talking strategy. And just when everyone looks ready and in position, the women pull on a rope.

Both of the cages fly open at the same time.

"What now?" I ask.

"RUN!" shouts Cyrus.

The Captain quickly turns to Tiko and slaps him in the face, which has the effect of four sugar free Red Bulls being poured down a funnel.

We skid out of the cage; girls do the same.

Immediately the kids send a volley of arrows in our wake, then launch into a chase. They scream, they laugh. Just another video game.

Instinctively, all of us sprint into the jungle, which hopefully will lead towards the beach and the boat. We merge with Melody and Cookie as we enter the jungle.

"Don't look back Cookie," warns the Captain. "These little rascals have great cardio."

We're not used to running barefoot in the jungle. Tears stream down Cookie's face. Small droplets of rain on a speeding car. Destination unknown.

The darkness of the canopy provides cover, and the kids slow down. Is this part of the game?

We find the Ocean Eyes sitting on the beach. Luckily, untouched. And together in a last group effort, we manage to push the catamaran into the water, sending it gliding into the calm blue lagoon waters.

We help Tiko aboard then we finally collapse on the teak deck. The ship slides towards the safety of the open water. We all look back in the direction of Parrot Island as the Captain lowers the anchor at a comfortable distance.

Melody pulls Cookie closer, wrapping an arm and a blanket around her.

Even as we float a thousand yards away, we can still hear the Albino's screams of agony escaping the jungle.

27

A Storm is Coming

Cookie is crushing morphine pills that she mixes into a glass of water. In a feat of denial about her boyfriend's capture, she springs into full nurturing mode as she vows to salvage what's left of Tiko.

"Pour it into my eyes," jokes Tiko, sweating and shivering while lying on the war room couch. "Seriously, what's the quickest way of absorption?" he asks.

"You don't want to know," Cookie winks. "Swallow this, and then, I'll shoot you with the antibiotics."

Tiko does.

"And I'm afraid your stitches are due next," the medic adds. "Not gonna be pretty. I gotta warn you."

If Tiko keeps shaking like this, his spine is gonna snap. He grabs a rum bottle that was squeezed between the cushions of the couch. Leftovers. He chugs at least three fingers.

I'm amazed at how Cookie is handling the situation. I hover behind her as she begins to work on my friend's shoulder.

"Look at you, with your little survival kit," I tell her, while she's holding a syringe full of penicillin. "A real doomsday *prepper*."

"Aren't we all prepping for the end?" she snags. "Some are just more *ready* than others."

I grab Tiko's hand.

"Hang in there, buddy," I tell him. He sinks comfortably into the cushions, thanks to the opiates his little heart is now pumping all the way into his four tentacles.

"Play with my hair, birdie," Tiko jokes. He's now on the level. "We are shoulder brothers now," he declares, hinting at my own stitches where the bullet was extracted a week ago.

Cookie signals Tiko to rest as she drops the needle on the metal tray. I've been hospitalized once, and there is some kind of an untold agreement with the nurses. Whenever they ask you to grade your level of pain, that's when you can put your finger on the scale. Hopefully they'll bring the good stuff.

Every hour or so since we've left the island, we hear the Albino screaming for his life. There are just no quits in him. Cookie should be terrorized, but somehow, the screaming gives her hope. He's still alive and kicking.

Their two hearts entangled. Suffering through spooky action at a distance.

The Captain steps into the war room with Melody. Turn by turn, he looks at each member of his crew, assessing the damages. You can tell he's already half-way committed into a new bottle.

"What now?" I risk asking first.

"Where not going anywhere," he says, planting his feet firmly. "My plane is on that island," he says, pointing towards it.

"Hey, my man is on this island too!" Cookie argues.

The captain looks at her, while twisting his silver necklace between his fingers. "We'll figure something out. I promise."

Melody pulls me aside and leans into my ear. "Have you noticed?" shes asks.

"Noticed what?"

"Whenever Brad is about to tell a lie, he twists his necklace."

I make a mental screenshot.

Personally, I wouldn't wager too much on the Albino's chances of survival beyond the next sunset.

And when it comes to the treasure, I don't know. We could just sail away while we can. We got millions in the coffers. Why bother?

This is no longer about adventure. This is greed. That's something I feel the Captain chose to trade along the way.

More screams come from the jungle. We all pretend we didn't hear.

The Captain brings our attention to one of the navigation monitors mounted in the war room. Not an expert here, but there's lots of red lines on that screen.

"Gang, we have another problem," Captain Brad announces rather calmly. We all gather to look at the satellite images.

"A storm is coming."

28

Cabin Fever

"Rats! Rats on board!"

That was the Captain. His voice comes deep from his quarters. What is he talking about? Is he talking about us? I'm getting paranoid.

Tiko and I are bunked in the opposite sled of the catamaran. Still, we can hear the Captain drenched in a drunken stupor.

"He's coconut," Tiko snarks. "Close your mind."

"Not much to do on this raft, except to go on a candlelight bender. I give him that," I acknowledge.

Before losing it, the Captain gave the order to shut off all the lights and electronics in an attempt to save what's left of the battery. Solar charging is not an option at the moment, due to the growing storm. Plus, we've been saving whatever is left of our emergency fuel in case we need to propel out of dodge, if the situation escalates.

In the dark, I wonder if the Albino has told the Captain. About Melody andmeI at Bonkers Fest. About our moment under the sunset. I wonder if that's the reason he's raging right now.

About that kiss.

We're all going mad. I'm afraid.

Super sets of waves rock the boat constantly. Through the small porthole, the sky grows darker even though it's just the middle of the afternoon.

"Aren't you scared?" I ask Tiko, laying in the bunk bed below me. He's doing better now. At least, I'm not alone in the dark.

"Scared? Birdie, I was on the brink of death yesterday. We had a little chat. The reaper let me go," he explains. "This is all bonus now."

I guess I'm in there too. Bonus time. I got shot. Almost drowned at *La Piscina*. And yesterday, those arrows flew really close. There might be a limit to our luck.

"All of our lives, we brush up against death. Over at least a thousand times. And with every single encounter, we manage to escape its claws. We do this until that day and that moment, where we just won't. Simple as that."

And I feel like I've wasted half of my life moving my car.

More drunken echoes coming from the Captain's quarters.

"Selfish rats!" the Captain repeats. This time, he sends furniture flying or something. Glass breaking.

"Screw it, I'm cheating," I tell Tiko, pulling out the PlayStation Portable from under my pillow. Firing up the cowboy game. The small screen lights up under the sheets.

I miss her so much right now.

The satellite was kept online and sends signal for navigation purposes, so I hitch a ride into my digital world. Escaping from one window into another.

On my digital white horse, I gallop across the open plains until I reach the forest. Then I follow the river up to the waterfall. I look around to make sure no other players can see me. Then I pull the rocks in the right sequence, revealing the entrance of our secret cavern.

It's been too long, baby. I'm sorry.

Everything is exactly as I left it. Safe behind the waterfall. The pot on the stove, the chair by the haystacks, the trinkets on the table.

The note she left me, next to that impenetrable chest. And inside, her last gift. Her little heart. Protected. And me, forever locked out.

There's a knock on the door of the cabin, and immediately, I shut down the device and shove it under my pillow. It's Melody.

"Guys, the Captain wants every soul in the war room. Now," she announces. "He has requested *a vote*."

Tiko grabs the lantern before we follow Melody onto the upper deck. The light is dim, but I can see a purple mark on her neck. Some kind of bruise? Jesus. Did Captain Brad lash out at her? Is he going nuts?

I won't let him put another finger on her. I feel powerless. But I'll do what it takes. Yes. I'll do what it takes.

Cyrus and Cookie are already present in the war room. The Captain is there too, holding a velvet hat upside down. You can tell Cookie has been sad. She's usually pretty stoic, but when she cries, it pours.

The Captain is stumbling a bit, but he manages to pull himself together. Vital functions.

"Members of the crew, I invoke a vote," starts the Captain, now that we're all accounted for. "All equal shares, all equal votes."

At least he remembers the code.

Cyrus passes around small pieces of paper and pencils.

"Yet before we render a decision, it is my job as the elected Captain to provide you all with the facts," he continues, bringing our attention once again to the satellite monitor.

"The storm has been boiling up, and we're right on its path. This morning, it crushed the southern tip of the Dominican Republic. And now that the eye of the storm has reached the Gulf stream, it will only pick up more steam. Turks & Caicos authorities are broadcasting messages to the population, asking to brace themselves for a Category 4 hurricane."

Cookie begins to weep again. She knows what this vote means. For us. For the expedition, and ultimately, for the Albino.

"On those pieces of paper, I want you to write down whether we should STAY for another day or LEAVE within the next hour."

Stay or leave.

I look at Tiko. He looks as clueless as I am. Is this some elaborate test of loyalty? Do we really have a say about this?

We all proceed to cast our votes into the black hat. Everyone is doing their best to avoid eye contact with Cookie. It's not a hard choice to be honest. For the Captain to forfeit his plane, this storm must look pretty bad.

The Captain counts the tally.

"Votes are 5 LEAVE and 1 STAY," he announces rather dryly. "It is settled then. Michael and Tiko, come help me roll down and deploy the sail. We'll have to save up that precious fuel for the worst-case scenario."

Tiko and I nod.

The Captain keeps going. "We'll sail around Parrot Island by the north-east side, and then, I'll chart a straight line to the Atlantic. Hopefully that monster will *banana* into the Gulf of Mexico."

Cookie erupts with more tears, then dashes away into the kitchen.

In his journal, the Captain crosses out the name of the Albino. Melody gives me an intricate look. Do I sense a relief?

The Albino is gone. And with him, our secret.

As Tiko and I follow the Captain up to the main deck, I halt for a second, standing still in the kitchen doorway.

"I'm sorry Cookie..." I tell her earnestly.

"It's not fair," she simply says. "Close the door now, I would like to cry."

I regroup with the boys on the top floor to prepare for departure. Immediately, the gushing wind throws me off balance the moment I step on the outside deck. The Captain's black hat flies off into the distance.

Up the sixty-foot mast, the wind blows strong, producing strange flares of blue lights that sparkle at the very top.

"Ah! St-Elmo's fire!" the Captain rejoices, reaching for the ropes. He's getting excited. Somehow, he must believe this is *him* against the elements. A grand display of delusional bravado.

That glow on top of the masthead is produced by an extreme buildup of electrical charge. I've read about this. This phenomena is known as St. Elmo's Fire. This also means lightning may strike the mast at any moment.

But the Captain remains untroubled.

"I've been hit by lightning once," he casually says.

That kind of explains a lot.

"It was a little after graduation. It was that summer we were all quoting Fight Club," the Captain recounts, while throwing the loose ropes at us. "I had this student job, picking up golf balls at the driving range."

Below the main sail, Tiko is turns the swivel while I pull the lever to raise up the anchor.

"Rain was pouring like hell, and I was in a small rowboat in the middle of the driving pond, finishing up gathering the pearls with a net."

Gusts of winds instantly fill up the deployed sail. Endowing our vessel with the power to fend the forty-foot waves incessantly rolling over.

"That's when it happened," continues the Captain, his face lit up, lifting a finger up in the air. "In the middle of the small lake. One big strike, and it fell right into the water next to me. I fell into the rowboat, and everything went white for a second. On that dark afternoon, I know I was spared."

The heavy rain is now pouring sideways. We should take cover.

29

The Death of Tiko

Our attempt at escaping the storm was futile.

We burned all the rocket fuel trying to propel The Ocean Eyes up around Parrot Island, only to be caught by the hurricane. And now the monster intensifies by the minute.

The champagne of storms.

We must be a hundred nautical miles up north. Well, it's hard to tell since we're totally sailing blind. All the power is out, all instruments went dark a couple of hours ago.

Our ship rendered to a multi million dollar raft.

The Captain does what he can to keep the ship straight. One hand on the wheel, the other on the bottle. And we're gliding down another giant slope like we're on a magic carpet. Every single swing brings the deck upward to an almost vertical position. I've always thought the pendulating pirate ship ride at the street fair was somehow exaggerated. Trust me, it's not.

Tiko and I struggle to fight the winds. With his bright yellow raincoat, Tiko keeps blinking on and off. Disappearing from my depth of field every time another wave washes across the bridge. It's pure chaos. And he's totally clumsy with his injured shoulder.

"Boys, we're flying!" screams the Captain brightly, fending the air from his post at the helm. Feeling strong from his booze armor.

We're already down to a half-sail, and yet, I feel that this violent wind is probably more than we can take. I know The Ocean Eyes was designed to sustain such brutality, complete with its aluminum frame and mast, but hear me out, I have a feeling it only looked good on paper. Right now, we are being crushed. With the bow making all sorts of noises.

"Captain, look! Starboard," shouts Tiko, with his bad hand holding his yellow hood in place, his good hand clenched to the railing.

"Hell Mary-Joseph..." gasps the Captain.

At the right side of the ship, maybe two hundred yards and closing in fast, a waterspout building up. That's a water tornado. Gathering tons of water into a spiral that goes all the way up to the clouds.

"Oh my god! Captain, what do we do?" I shout towards the

wheel.

"Boys shut down that sail! NOW!" he orders screaming, as the ship rocks from side to side.

I'm escalating the bridge towards Tiko's position. He struggles with the ropes and swivels. The deck is so slippery. Visibility, almost null.

"What's going on?" I shout against the heavy rain washing on our faces constantly.

"Too much pressure! The wind is blowing up the sail, and I can't shut it," Tiko shouts back. "There's nothing we can do with those ropes."

Physics doesn't care about your feelings.

Some huge wave punches us from the right. We both slide on the open deck, our hands trying to grasp anything to avoid being washed overboard. Then we both slowly crawl back towards the swivel.

"Boys!" screams the Captain. "I can't hold her any longer!"

Tiko pulls out his pocketknife and clenches it between his teeth.

"You gotta be kidding me," I shout into his face.

But he immediately reaches for the ropes circling the boom and begins to slice back and forth like a mad man.

One rope, two ropes, three ropes.

Finally, the sail gets loose and releases all the tension. We immediately feel the ship slowing down. The rocking becomes somehow manageable.

That's when the boom—now free from the ropes—swings back across the deck to slam Tiko right in the chest. Picking him up like a leaf. Now fused together, they quickly fly to the opposite side of the ship.

I watch my friend dangling over the water, both arms wrapped around the slippery beam. Hungry waves keep reaching up from under his feet.

"Hold on! I'm coming!" I shout.

I can clearly see how he's struggling with his shoulder. The pain must be insane.

"I can't!" he shouts back, the waves now nibbling at his soles. Shoes are long gone.

I run to the left side of the ship, but he's dangling way too far above the water for me to reach him with my bare hands, or even a pole.

"It's okay, Birdie...it's okay. It's all a bonus anyways, remember?"

"No!" I scream at him.

A second later, a giant wave rolls from the right, and I lose sight of Tiko for a moment. I wipe the salty rain from my face, and he reappears. Still out there, clenched to the boom.

Then a wall of water comes rolling in.

Tiko looks into my eyes one last time.

"Bye bye, Birdie."

The ocean finally opens its mouth to gobble my best friend. And when the water recedes, there's nothing left.

Today, Tiko was not spared.

30

Into the Abyss

In his journal, the Captain crosses out the name of yet another crew member. His name was Tiko, and he was my best friend.

Sometimes the best books don't get returned.

I begin to understand what Tiko meant on that first day: When he said *it doesn't really matter where we all came from.* What mattered, was that we were all here, *now.*

Tiko looked at you and saw the most recent version of yourself. Without the luggage, the money nor the scars.

Valuing people solely based on their creative output and on the kindness they show towards each other.

They told him I was a DJ, and he introduced me to others just as such. Never embarrassed by my naive attempts. Sails fully bloated with hope for the future.

The Oceans Eyes has now been rendered totally inoperable. With no more fuel, power nor rudder. The rest of the crew hunkers inside its bowels.

All waiting for the worst.

Most of the dishes are broken into a million pieces and keep sliding on the wet floors as we sway from side to side.

None of that matters anymore.

This ship is going down.

31

Castaways

By some miracle, Rhe Ocean Eyes survived the storm. And so did we.

She beached herself softly on a random shoreline in the early hours of the morning. The Captain has no idea where we ended up. We've drifted all night. Probably down south along the island chain. Or maybe this is Antarctica? Who knows.

The black volcanic sand burns under my feet.

Birds circle me on the beach. The tiny ones, sprinting so fast you can't even see their legs. None of them fear me. I find it unusual. Are we really here? Or are we dead, and this is just a final rendering?

Or maybe after spending a certain amount of time in nature, you harmonize. Sync up. Back to the root of existence.

Primal numbers.

The Captain and most of the crew, to be honest, drank like it was our last night on earth. Now Mr. Hangover wants his payback. And it's brutal.

The boat has no power, satellite nor sail. It's been basically rendered a grotesque raft with luxury finishes. And forget about the Japanese toilets. We've been blown back to the bucket age.

Without electricity, the food is gonna go bad within hours. And we'll probably have to fight over whatever snacks Cookie managed to stash away.

In the cloud, we have all the money in the world and yet, not a single grocery store for hundreds of nautical miles around.

This beach is beautiful though. Five stars.

"Where do we go when we die, Cyrus?" I ask our shaman walking by my side and who has remained silent up to now. Deep into his morning contemplation. He lights up.

"Ah, the big question! You are wondering about your friend?" he asks softly.

"I don't know. We got lucky. Ending up here in one piece. Maybe Tiko pulled some favors up there or something?" I ask Cyrus, fishing for some deeper knowledge.

"Everything is energy. Our bodies, mere vessels," he explains. "And when we die, that energy goes back to the universe. Where it all came from."

Makes sense. And quite simple.

"Now when it comes to miracles, so to speak, I don't believe the dead have any powers over the material world. Or maybe they can nudge a cloud once in a while. Maybe send us a sign here and there."

Well. Whatever happened last night, we were spared. We were all spared.

The Captain and Cookie catch up on the beach. Captain Brad throws one of the rusty swords to Cyrus. He catches it swiftly.

"Here. Start to hatchet. Cookie will help you. You guys need to build a giant bonfire. And then you keep it burning and smoking all day. You understand me? This will signal our position."

They both nod.

"It's important because Micheal and I will take a little hike and scale that cliff over there. Try to get the lay of the land. We're about to find out if we're all gonna die here."

The Captain scoops two bottles of rum that he salvaged from the outside minibar. There is no escaping his demons.

"How about some water?" I ask him bluntly.

"There's plenty of coconuts out there," he shrugs. Then turns to the catamaran.

"Melody, can you assess the electronics while we're gone? See if you can salvage the solar panels and maybe if we are lucky, reconnect with the outside world."

"Yes, my Captain," she nods before sending me a wink.

"Worst case, we have the radio," Cookie says. "There's a cargo ship route crossing the Gulf Stream, if we broadcast every hour, someone might pick up our position."

"Good," the Captain says. "You all have your orders. Let's go, jungle boy. I smell some fresh bananas downwind."

He doesn't smell shit.

"Micheal, a moment before you go?" Melody shouts from the main deck. I climb up, and she pulls me under the awning, behind the outdoor kitchen pantry.

"What's up?" I ask her, standing inches away from her freckles with a mischievous smile.

"Not now, Michael. Look," she shushes, as she opens up the Captain's journal. She probably sneaked it out of their quarters.

In his journal, the Captain has crossed out yet another name from the list of the expedition.

This time, it's my name.

32

Doom Cliffs

Where is he gonna do it?

We've hiked along the bluffs for two hours, and now that bonfire is just a tiny speck in the distance. With a tall stack of smoke rising up to the heavens. A tiny lifeline that still connects us back to the crew.

Is he gonna strike me in the back of the head?

With a bottle or maybe a big stick? Is he just gonna push me down the ravine? None of us packed any weapons. It's gonna have to be hand to hand combat. The question is simply *when?*

At this elevation, most of the terrain is covered with tall grass and white flowers. A few bushes here and there. We stop for a moment to gaze at the ocean. The captain swings the first empty bottle towards the horizon, and it disappears down the cliff into the crashing waves below.

Captain Brad is drunk. That's good for me.

He doesn't drink to forget, but to remember. That's a good moment to quiz him further. I'm still trying to put all the pieces together. About the plane crash. About his lost partner. About the treasure.

"Do you think Tyler is alive?" I ask.

"I don't know about Tyler, but the money is," he replies rather cryptically.

"What do you mean by that? *Alive?*"

"It's back on the ledger," he starts to explain. "We can't access the funds on our end, of course, we need the secret key. But somehow, the crypto wallet and its content has resurfaced on the blockchain. Most of the money is still there."

I'm totally shocked. Confused. The waves below seem to grow more violent.

"Jesus, how long have you known about this, Brad?"

"Two weeks maybe," the Captain grunts, looking in the distance while twisting the cork of the second rum bottle. He takes a big swig.

"Don't you think it's something the crew would have appreciated to know?" I fire back.

"Why? The treasure. That's what kept us going. Hasn't it?"

Looking around the bluffs, I realize there is nowhere to hide here. Is he gonna make a move now? Curious pelicans land here and there. At least some witnesses.

"Why are you telling me now, Brad?" I dare to ask him.

And there it is.

"Because it doesn't matter anymore, Michael. You are not coming back."

Here we go.

The Captain flips the bottle and launches at me, going for the head. I'm quick enough to dodge the swing and send the bottle flying away in the tall grass. Pelicans take off.

He kicks my leg, and we both roll onto the sand.

"I know about you and Melody!" he shouts, trying to control my arms, I kick all over the place. He's stronger than I thought.

"If I can't have her, neither will you!" he spits all over me. His face is purple with rage. Showing sharp teeth.

That's when I remember the marks on Melody's neck. And that gives me a second breath, fills me with purpose.

One kick in his ribs, and he's rolls over. Winded. He struggles to catch his breath for a moment, then quickly charges back, unphased.

"Lack of loyalty is something I can't tolerate on my expedition," he screams. And immediately, I wonder what he's gonna do to Melody the moment he comes down. I can't let that happen. This is no longer an option. This has to end here.

He grabs a branch and jumps over me once again, this time locking me in a chokehold with the wood piece under my neck. And he presses hard. Then harder.

"Won't let you have it! Won't let you have her," he shouts. "You've been asking all those questions since we've picked you up in Tulum..."

I'm gasping for air. My hands slither up his face, trying to push him away. But I'm fading fast.

"Don't you get it by now?" he whispers in my ear. "Don't you get it?"

The sky is spinning.

"The treasure. Tyler. The Fountain. These things, they're all the same!"

The curtain is falling. And at the last moment, I hear a thick sound.

The pressure from the wood branch is suddenly released and

the Captain somehow rolls to my side. I quickly glance to my left, and he's lying there, not moving.

And when I twist to my right, I discover the tail end of a yellow raincoat.

"Hello, birdie."

33

Over My Dead Body

Tiko stands there, holding the big rock he just smashed on the Captain's head, his other arm folded inside his mangled yellow raincoat.

"Oh my god! I thought you were dead!" I shout as I spring back to my feet.

"So did I," he starts. "Woke up this morning on the purest sands I've ever felt. I thought I was in heaven. But the pain quickly caught up," he explains, hinting at his shoulder.

He lets go of the rock.

"That's when I saw you two idiots scaling up the cliffs, so I decided to tail you for a bit," he adds. "And then you guys started to fight."

"What took you so long?" I ask, almost mad.

"I was looking for a nice rock, you know."

I try to go for a hug.

"Ahhhhhh," he says, struck with the pain.

We both turn to the Captain. I kneel down to inspect him. There's a bit of blood at the back of his head. I run a finger under his nose.

"He's out cold, but he's still breathing."

"What do we do?" Tiko asks, puzzled.

"My friend, there's a lot of things I will explain on the way back. But what you need to know right now is that this man...this man is really bad."

"Okay. And?"

One look at Tiko and he understands what's coming next. With one swift move, I pluck the silver necklace from under Brad's shirt and pocket it.

Together, we begin to roll his body towards the cliff. And together, we give him the final kick.

Memento mori, asshole. You will never find The Fountain.

34

Mutiny

Am I going to tell the others?

On the decision scale, I'm weighing pros and cons while I trail behind Tiko.

The money is alive. That's one thing. But with Brad gone, we wouldn't even know where to look. And screw Parrot Island. We're kinda blacklisted there. I twist and turn the silver necklace inside my pocket. As if it had any powers.

Maybe it's best to keep everything between me and the pelicans.

The smoke from the bonfire spirals up above the forest. We're about to dive back down under the canopy. Good thing, because the sun is killing me right now, and we haven't drink anything yet.

Tiko picks two ripe coconuts and smashes them on a sharp rock.

A short relief.

"What should we do now?" he asks, between sips. "And how's the boat?"

"It's a dead log," I tell him, emotionally detached.

The jungle is thick, and yet, no parrots here either. Those pelicans are probably picking Brad's pockets by now. Rot in hell buddy.

"Hopefully, Melody managed to radio some ship along the cargo route. But first, we need to fix you up, brother. That broken wing looks very bad."

"Let's pray that the Kraken didn't gobble all the morphine," Tiko says, worried about the pain. "That storm rocked us pretty hard. Did we lose anyone else?"

"Nah. I would have been next if the Captain had his way," I tell him.

"What did Brad tell you?" asks Tiko.

"Something about the money being back online, yet out of reach," I explain vaguely. "Right now, I can't think straight."

"So Tyler *did* survive the crash?" he continues.

But I remain silent. It doesn't really matter now. We'll never find that stupid plane.

As we exit the forest onto the beach, we stop in our tracks. In the distance, there are at least a dozen archers surrounding The Ocean Eyes.

"Oh no. Not again," exhales Tiko, taking two steps back and putting a hand on his shoulder. A souvenir from our last encounter with the previous tribe.

But it's too late, they spotted us. And among them, a familiar silhouette.

"Is that...the Albino?" we both exclaim at the same time. We sprint towards the boat. Oblivious to danger and the politics about to unfold.

"Seize them!" the Albino commands, waiting for Cyrus to translate his orders to the archers.

"How is that even possible?" Tiko whispers.

And that's when I get it. Everything falls into place. We're back. Back on Parrot Island. The storm must have pushed us in circles until we finally wrecked again on the northern tip on this unforgiving rock.

Unbelievable. The Albino is alive. I guess once in a while, one lucky particle gets to escape the black hole.

The archers surround us with their pointy tips. Meanwhile, Cookie is standing next to her man, arms wrapped around him, looking like Tarzan and Jane.

Upon a closer look, the Albino's skin is covered in bite marks and patched up wounds. Bandages on his legs and arms. And on his head, a folded-up bandana acts as an eye patch. It's a cool look for sure.

"Hum, good to see you Al," I try candidly.

"Shut up, Micheal!" he orders. "Screw all of you! You left me here for dead!" he shouts, towering above the archers. "Three days! Three excruciating days struggling in that forsaken pit!"

He spits on the ground, then looks at the sky. Regaining his poise.

Melody emerges from the sidelines, quickly covering her mouth as she notices Tiko standing next to me, alive and well. She dashes for the hug.

"Ahhhh," my Tiko mutters again in pain. But love prevails.

"What happened? They let you go?" I ask the Albino.

He just grunts. Is that a yes?

"The snake pit was a test, and he passed it," explains Cyrus. "And now the whole tribe is at his orders. He's the king of Parrot Island," says the interpreter, as the Albino lifts his chin, arms crossed on his chest.

"And you've fixed the sail! See! Everything is fine!" adds Tiko, trying to diffuse.

Up there on The Ocean Eyes, makeshift ropes Woven out of twisted vines are used to tie the sail back to the boom. The raft will float again.

"Wait, where is Brad?" Melody asks suddenly.

Silence.

Tiko and I both take a deep breath.

"He fell off a cliff." I side-eye Tiko, hoping he will stick to the narrative.

"Fell off a cliff?" repeats Melody. We can see the mix of emotions on her face. A big question mark.

Of course, nobody believes any of that.

"That's treachery! That's absolute, total bullshit. And sooner or later, one of you magpies will have to pay for this!" rages the Albino. We've never seen him this agitated. Let alone speak more than twelve words in a sequence.

"The term you are looking for here is *mutiny*," corrects Cyrus.

The Albino grunts again.

"Tie them up," he orders. "I'm the Captain now."

When the tide goes out, you get to see who wears the pants. That's Warren Buffet.

35

Standing On the Plank

It's been twenty-four hours since we killed the Captain.

With him dead, my share of the expedition should be about one million dollars.

But none of that matters now, because if I don't find something clever to say within the next thirty seconds, the crew will push Tiko and me to the end of this plank. Down into the ocean.

Our hands are tied, and I can feel the pointy tip of the sword against my back.

There is no land in sight, and earlier today, we spotted a dozen sharks circling the boat. They looked both hungry and bored. And I don't know what's worse.

Think Michael, think. What would the Captain say? Screw it

"I know where to find the treasure," I tell them, shouting over my shoulder.

In my hand, I squeeze the silver necklace.

36

Cargo Worship

The Albino keeps two archers on board as his personal security, even though we all agree the band was back together.

Except for Brad, who's been kicked out.

I guess trust is still an issue for the new Captain. Too many rats in the kitchen when the chef isn't looking.

Still, I got to admit, a little law and order is welcomed aboard. *La Pax Albina.*

We spent half of the day reshuffling the rooms. Melody had to forfeit the Captain's quarters. Cookie was crowned the new queen and took it over with the Albino.

Cyrus got pushed back in the bunks with Tiko, so freckles and I could move into the medium room together.

With just one bed.

As for the two archers, they perched their hammocks some-where on the upper deck. Stargazers. That's what they are. And while both of them are napping, all members of the expedition are assembled in the war room. Conspiring from inside the belly of the whale.

"They won't talk!" Cyrus says.

"Go ask them again! Ask them about the metal bird," the Albino pressures.

Everyone stares at the interpreter.

"Oh, they know about the plane crash. Trust me. They just won't lead us to it. They said it's sacred ground, apparently," explains Cyrus.

"What do you mean by *sacred?*" Melody asks.

I've read a story like that, somewhere. They called this *Cargo Worship.* In the article, some uncontacted tribe in the Pacific had witnessed a cargo plane crashing onto their island. That plane was filled with war supplies, dry food and mysterious technology.

So the next thing you know, the tribe began to worship the cargo plane and its broken fuselage. Feeling they were blessed by the many gifts it provided, and praying every day for more favors to rain from above.

"What if we kill one of them and make the other watch?" Cookie asks, deadpanned.

"That's not how we operate," says the Albino with a subtle smile. You know he also thought about it.

Tiko keeps fidgeting with a pen. *Click, click, click.*

"Stop that, would you?" Cookie lashes out. "You drive me nuts. Want more morphine?"

Cyrus brushes his beard. "I have an idea," he says, as he's diving inside of his jacket pocket. He pulls out the small flask we stole back in *La* Cárcel. The one filled with scopolamine. He places it on the table in front of us.

Colombian Devil's Breath, baby.

"I remember a newscast where the reporters volunteered to go under the influence. A pinch of that vile powder was blown into their faces. Ten minutes later, they were both emptying their apartments into a moving truck at the request of the producer," recounts Cyrus.

Everybody remains silent. Wondering.

"They did it for hours, with no questions asked. No inhibitions, nothing. Zombie mode activated," the shaman continues.

"You think they would take us to the metal bird if we asked gently? After we blow them a little kiss from the devil?" Cookie asks.

"It's worth a try," decides the Albino.

We all seem to agree.

"Let's pack light," orders the new Captain. "We will leave at dawn. Everyone."

37

Jungle Expedition

Here we are, pointing the two archers forward like a source stick. Cyrus had a pretty good idea, I have to admit. The two short men are leading the pack, machete in hand and slashing out a path through the thick ferns.

The expedition is out of range from the satellite dish, meaning we have to rely solely on these two human GPS's. They don't seem to care whether they step on slicing volcanic rocks nor poison ivy. Their foot skin is totally callous. Plus, the scopolamine is supposed to remove all sense of fear and incredulity.

I'm trailing behind the Albino, with Melody by my side. So many cobwebs we have to fend through. I believe spiders keep a ledger about how many of them you've killed over the years. And whenever you decide to go camping, they pull out their notes for revenge. Thinking about it, I'm glad we spared that big one back in the Cuckoo's Nest.

That day seems so distant now. So comfortable. And look at us now, chasing the ghost of a man named Tyler and his crashed plane.

Here is a list of things that can kill you in the jungle:

1 - Jaguars, tigers, cougars and anything else that goes *grrrr*.

2 - A coconut crab alone cat cut your foot off.

3 - Touching a giant hogweed plant will melt your skin within minutes.

4 - Quick sand, apparently not just for video games.

5 - Malaria, Dengue fever, Zika and arrogance.

Cyrus halts the train. "Hold on guys, it's time to renew their prescription," he says, hinting at the two guides.

The shaman moves along towards the head of the pack. He carefully pinches a little dust from the flask then blows it into the archers' faces, renewing their vows. And our expedition can resume.

Yet not so long after that, our two zombie guides are suddenly facing a wall. Literally. A forty feet steep rock-face the two archers now prepare to scale. They both sheath their machetes into their vine belts and just go for it.

"No way," exhales Tiko, rubbing his bad shoulder.

"Just mimic their climbing holds," the Albino says. "They'll show you the path of least resistance."

We boost Melody up first, followed by Tiko and his broken wing. Then it's me, Cyrus and the Albino, who promised to catch us if we slip.

Halfway up our ascension, Cyrus pushes a muted scream. And then we hear it. The glass tube containing the Devil's breath shatters on the rocks down below. And that's the end of it. Meanwhile, the two guides keep climbing, undisturbed.

"How long do we got?" asks the Albino, always calm and pragmatic.

"Two hours, maybe?" the shaman says. "Then it will eventually wear off. We must be near the wreckage by now, judging by our altitude."

"The sun will set soon guys," warns Melody, already atop of the cliff and looking over the jungle towards the horizon.

This is about to get interesting. What happens when the Devil's breath wears off? I guess we're about to find out.

38

The Cavern

Our shelter for the night is a three star rental you won't find anywhere online. A small cavern nestled atop the rock wall. Hard to find. Still, amazingly, someone was here before us.

There is a fire pit, a few empty water bottles and lots of blood covered bandages scattered around a first aid kit. That blood is not fresh though, darkened. Could be months old.

"That's a safety kit for a Cessna," Cookie says, reading the box. "You think that was Tyler's?"

"Definitely," Melody clarifies. "He must have come down from the mountain, spending the night here, tending to his wounds. We're on the right track, people."

Tiko pushes the bandages aside with his foot and sits on the big log. He starts to assemble tinder and dried bark into a stack.

"He was hurt," Tiko mutters.

"But alive!" brightens Melody.

The two archers have been standing there *on idle* for a moment. There must be less than an hour remaining on the minuter before we're cooked.

"What do we do with *them*?" I ask the Albino.

"I got this. We'll go for a little sunset walk," he winks, wrapping his arm around the archers' shoulders to slowly guide them outside the cave. As you would bring seniors to the bingo.

"You're just gonna whack them?" Tiko asks.

Al wouldn't do that. It's against his code. Plus, if we kill one, they'll multiply.

"I'll throw the ball far enough, so they don't bring it back," explains the Albino, rather cryptic.

Cookie digs into the ration backpack and hands me a cold beer. "Here. That's our only one. Enjoy it while it's cold. The ice pack has all melted."

I take a first generous sip and pass the bottle around to Tiko.

"See, the first sip feels too tight, too cold," he says, pointing at the bottle's neck. He then takes a swig. "The second sip, on the other hand, is just perfect. Right temp, good flow."

"Is that a metaphor for something?" I ask.

"Life, birdie!" he simply says, circling the bottle towards Melody. "Between childhood and sickness, you get twenty years of peace."

He's right.

"What are you gonna do with the money?" Melody asks. "That's *if* the money is still up there, of course."

We all reflect in silence for a moment.

"Don't really know, to be honest. That was not our journey to begin with. I was just looking for freedom, you know?" I explain.

"Yeah, I start to believe this stupid treasure is cursed," Tiko claims. "Maybe we're better off not touching it. Like the Ark of the Covenant."

I have this feeling too.

"Besides, what more do you want? Steaks for lunch?" Tiko continues.

He takes another sip as the bottle boomerangs and then smiles, looking into the fire Cookie has just lit. "I remember my first job interview. Showed up to this restaurant with no resume. I picked three lemons from the bar and started juggling for the manager. I was hired as a dishwasher on the spot."

That summer money was everything. We got all we needed,

really. A little beer, a little weed. Bikes to go around and meet the girls. Predrink in the parking lot *en route* to a house party in the suburbs.

"The good life!" Cookie says.

"Feels like we're gonna work the rest of our lives trying to go back to that level of carefreeness," Tiko continues.

"One thing for sure, we're blacklisted anywhere there's a Cartel presence," I remind Tiko. "So what's the plan if we jump ship?'

"We have to go north, birdie. Winter kills all mosquitoes."

I made the decision not to tell anybody about the money *back online.* After all, God knows what we're gonna find inside of that plane. Maybe our next clue? Something to keep their hopes up. That's what Brad was looking for.

"I'm gonna hit the sack," Cookie says. "Don't you wake me up unless the monster has finished eating one of you."

39

Metal Bird

Sun flares. They tickle my face as my eyelids slowly open.

Cyrus is already up and stands at the mouth of the cavern, his tall silhouette projected on the rock walls behind me. He's awfully quiet. He does that most mornings. Some sort of sun worshiper. I go meet him in the light.

"What did you ask for today?" I ask our shaman.

"You can't ask for anything, that's not how it works."

I stay silent, waiting for Cyrus to spill the rest of his dogma.

"You just say thank you for the things you've got. The things that you've found. You know? You take inventory. You stand there, head up and basking into the light."

We both take a deep breath. Exhale.

"And then, if you pay attention, the universe is gonna show you where to look."

Interesting. Maybe we're all here because the universe likes so much to look at itself. Reflecting that light.

As the sun rises and the curtain slowly rolls up the valley, the panorama goes from grayscale to bright colors. And in the jungle green, something unusual glitters in the distance. Golden and red likes pieces of a broken mirror.

"There's your metal bird," points Cyrus.

In my chest, my heart pumps its fist.

Finally, a clue.

"Everybody, wake up!" I shout at the group lined up around the fire pit. "We've located the plane."

The news has the effect of a double espresso stabbed in their thighs with an EpiPen.

Five minutes later, we're all packed and moving. Slashing and slashing our way across the valley. Closing in on that pot of gold at the end of a two-week rainbow.

Even though I know for a fact that the treasure itself won't be in that wreck, thanks to Brad, I'm equally excited to catch a glimpse at this pirate ghost we've been chasing.

Tyler where are you?

"Look, up there, that's the tail!" Tiko says with excitement, waving his machete and rushing towards the fuselage.

Just as Cyrus had explained back in the village, the locals turned the whole crash site into a holy ground. The whole area has been cleared out. The broken parts of the fuselage are assembled together on the ground. Pieces of a puzzle, which they've never seen the box.

Like those dinosaurs in the Museum of Paris.

The seats have been salvaged and erected in front of the metal bird to act as a throne, decorated with flower offerings and incense. A row of red Jerry cans form a semi-circle around the thrones.

The whole attempt looks naive and beautiful.

"Do you think Tyler found his way out of Parrot Island?" Melody asks.

"Not if the archers found him first," Tiko dreads.

"Hey, maybe they helped him out, you know?" Cyrus suggests. "The man who fell from the sky."

The Albino sortssorts through a pile of rubbish. There is a bit of blood in the cockpit. Broken glass. Yet, no sign of the waterproof case that might have contained the crypto wallet.

If Tyler survived, he took it with him. No doubt about that. And that would explain why the money ultimately found its way back online. Back on the blockchain.

"Melody!" Cookie shouts. "Over here."

Over a broken wing propped up as a table, Cookie unfolds a map.

Tyler's map.

"That looks like his flight plan," Melody explains upon looking at the topographic lines, and runs a finger over the different pencil markings.

"Seems like he was planning on landing in Havana. So Brad was right in that sense," she explains. "But my opinion is that it was only for refueling purposes." She keeps running her finger along the faint pencil line that continues flying across the Gulf. "See that? His final destination was Panama City."

The whole crew gets excited again.

"So what's in Panama?" Tiko asks.

"Lots of shade," replies Cookie.

Meanwhile, Cyrus who went back to sort through the debris, manages to pull out some sort of brochure. He slaps it on the evidence table.

"This might have something to do with it?" Cyrus says, showing us the leaflet that reads BANK OF PANAMA.

"Wait. This logo looks familiar," I think out loud. "I've seen it somewhere else."

Digging deep in my pocket, I pull out the silver necklace. The one I plucked from Brad's neck before rolling him down the cliff. And there it was. The same tiny logo from the brochure engraved on the back of the silver pendant.

This is not a necklace. It's a key.

III

ACT THREE

Don't forget to feed the monster.

40

To Panama City

Turns out the Panama Canal is very rich in deposits.

Kings, Queens and soccer players, among others, have been stashing money down there for decades. Propping up an elaborate network of corporate attorneys, investment bankers and shady real estate developers.

Everywhere, shiny towers reaching for the heavens and built for people who don't pray anymore.

The Ocean Eyes has been speeding west ever since we found Tyler's map. Parrot Island is now far in our rear-view mirror. And we all promised we'd never set foot on this cursed rock again.

If you picture The Americas as a giant hourglass, Panama City is that small waist right in the middle. The funnel where all the grains of sand converge through.

Give it enough time and a couple of Hollywood accounting tricks, and you can ultimately flip the whole thing over.

Making all cash anew.

Fresh funds available to build more sandcastles.

We believe that's where Tyler buried the treasure. Somewhere deep down in the vault of The Bank of Panama.

It took us a minute of researching online to figure out what the silver key on the necklace was all about. It provides anonymous access to a safe deposit box to whoever holds it in his possession. These keys apparently are issued by the bank in pairs. Therefore, both Tyler and Brad must have had their own.

Of course, with the way cryptocurrencies work, we don't really expect to find gold bars nor US paper stacks in that deposit box. But hopefully, we can retrieve the password to the digital wallet. A way to access the treasure and move the funds around as we please.

As the Captain told me before his unfortunate demise, the funds are somehow back online. Alive and fluctuating in sync with the markets. Most probably the work of Tyler who managed to extract himself from the jungle in one piece.

The Albino stands up in the war room, hands on his hips and looking at the map displayed on the navigation system. The snake bites are healing well, yet I'm afraid the eye patch will be a permanent look. More power to him.

"There's no way we can approach the coast of Panama without getting detected and boarded by customs officers. This is way too close to the grid for comfort," he explains, fishing for ideas.

"And The Ocean Eyes has been described in many articles after that stunt we pulled at the music festival," Cookie adds. "This time we won't fool anyone with a bumper sticker on the back."

"We're a ghost ship from now on," says the Albino.

Legendary. We all reflect for a moment.

"What if we ship ourselves in banana containers?" Tiko starts. Not a bad idea.

"Can't do," Cookie quickly darts off. "You'll either suffocate to death from the heat or freeze into a Häagen-Dazs bar if you pick a refrigerated cargo."

We can't blame Tiko for brainstorming.

"I have an idea," Melody goes. "What about a cruise ship?"

"You mean to *sneak* aboard a moving cruise ship?" the Albino wonders.

"We don't have to go full pirate. We could just buy a ticket," Melody explains, as she unfolds her laptop in front of us. She performs a quick search for cruises departing from the

Caribbean.

We all get closer.

"Here we go," she exclaims, starting to read from the advertisement. "The Majestic Liner promises a six-day escape across the blue. Departing from Belize with stops in Colombia, Panama City, and Guatemala."

"That could work," the Albino says. Belize is a shit show anyways. We could approach their country on a battleship, for all they care."

"What do we say, people?" Melody asks the Albino. "We could hop on that carousel, do a merry-go-round until you guys pick us back up a week later."

"Works for me," he replies. "We'll get the dinghy ready for drop off as soon as we arrive."

A plan is taking shape.

"And that layover in Panama City gives us, what? Eight hours on land at best? That should be plenty of time to find the right bank and check on that safe deposit box."

Looks like we're all set. And I've never been on a corporate cruise. I mean, this thing looks nice for a 40,000-gallon septic tank drifting from port to port.

The Albino gives the go ahead to purchase the tickets. "So

here's how it will go," he instructs. "Micheal and Melody are gonna play a nice newlywed couple. So let's book them a honeymoon suite."

Melody gives me a side eye. Thank you, God.

"Meanwhile, for support, Cyrus and Tiko will play two frat kids on a booze cruise. You guys will need to keep an eye on them. Cause a distraction if you need to."

"Mommy, you gonna watch me go down the water slide?" Tiko jokes to Melody.

Fun week ahead.

"You'll miss my food guys, I'll tell you that," Cookie laughs. "Anything cooked aboard these ships is battered in gutter oil."

Under the table, Melody puts a hand on my knee.

41

Hitching a Ride on The Majestic Liner

Like most baby boomers, my parents have less money than they pretended to. That's why they keep washing their cars every Sunday morning, so they look brand new. And we can't blame them. They're proud of their things.

Ever since they retired, my father tends to see their life savings as a block of Parmesan cheese. And every day, my parents must open the fridge to scratch a little bit off the top. Never to be replenished.

Oh, the agony.

Maybe that's why they always liked this idea of a cruise ship vacation. A predetermined amount. A clear timeline. Food vouchers. Everything in one place. The ship is moving, so you don't have to.

Going through life on a lazy river.

This whole idea kinda repulses me. Clinging like a flea to these mammoths of the sea. Bluntly oozing from artificial beach to artificial beach. Entering every town through the gift shop. A facade they put up just for you.

Did you know that the average passenger of a cruise will gain ten pounds per week?

Anyways. I gotta take this next week as an experiment. Plus, the honeymoon suite doesn't look too shabby.

Speaking of which.

"Tiko wants us to join them at the buffet," Melody says, as she enters our cabin in a stunning swimsuit I haven't seen before. Did she enjoy a little onboard shopping?

A cruise ship will generate on average an extra million dollars per day with retail and upsells of all kinds.

"How's my material girl? Listen, I need to talk to you," I tell her.

"Oh, please don't propose, Michael. It's too soon," she replies, as she faceplants on the bed.

I smile.

Did you know that two thousand five hundred weddings take place on cruise ships annually?

"Baby, looks like we're pretty much all set," I tell her, spreading my arms to showcase the honeymooners package. Complete with daily pastry baskets. That's $10k a day we plucked straight from the expedition coffers.

"No. It's about what happened last year," I tell her, now looking serious and holding the PSP in my hand. "I' never really gave my ex-girlfriend a proper send off. You know? And I think it's a bit unfair to you, to be honest."

Melody smiles, stays silent.

She's been very kind to me over the last couple of weeks. And now, it appears clear that both of our hearts are really into it.

My ex-girl might be gone, but *that feeling* came back somehow. Call it the return of love. Wrapped in a different person, yet, same feeling.

Grabbing Melody's hand, I pull her towards the balcony. Yes, we have a private balcony. And outside in silence, while facing the ocean breeze, I look one last time at the playable device. The screen is dark. I close my eyes, give it a kiss and throw it overboard, down crashing into the ocean.

Of course, my heart will go on.

Melody wraps her arm around my neck, gives me a peck on the cheek.

I no longer need to know what's inside that chest. This

obsession, finally gone. I'm at peace knowing that before she left, my ex put something in there just for me. And that it will remain safe inside from now until forever.

42

Beyond the Sea

The cruise ship buffet has a karaoke machine, and Tiko gladly offered himself as a tribute to take part in tonight's entertainment.

"Nobody really likes karaoke," I tell Melody.

"Nobody likes a grump!" she counterstrikes.

Touché-coulé.

The crew gave Tiko a flamenco shirt and a sailor hat. He's to the moon. And he sings the Bobby Darin's chorus to the synth.

Somewhere beyond the sea
  Somewhere waiting for me
  My lover stands on golden sands
  And watches the ships that go sailing

He probably thinks it's from *The Little Mermaid.*

"Our friend is an idiot," Melody laughs while clapping.

"Tiko is special, we need to protect him."

"He's so dumb, we need to water him twice a week," Cyrus adds, as Tiko strolls down the carpeted stairs under a round of applause.

The dining area has cosmic carpets. Same pattern you can find in city buses. Did you know that all cruise ships are required to have a morgue on board? As they say, the show must go on.

I sit down with a giant plate of Lobster and a Caesar salad. The calorie count is close to four thousand.

"What if I stood up and screamed *iceberg*, right now?" Tiko asks, facing a double deck lasagna with a side of sour creamed baked potatoes. Calorie count: one million.

They would probably lock him up in the drunk tank. And that's not an upgrade.

"Cookie just sent me a message," Melody starts. "She found this guy online. He calls himself The Falcon. Says he can craft some fake IDs for all of us before we land in Panama City."

"Why would we need fake IDs?" Tiko asks, going Godzilla on the lasagna.

"The bank will want some sort of log entry," Melody explains. "Sure, the silver key is anonymous and so is the number of the deposit box. But these banks have high security. And we will need to pass the lobby level."

Makes sense, acknowledges Cyrus, waving a crab leg like a magic wand. Calorie count: who cares?

"The Falcon, you said?" I push forward.

"Yup. He wants us to catch him at 10 a.m. sharp on a street corner. Somewhere just outside of the downtown core."

"*Catch* him?" Tiko asks. Pulling out his phone, he starts browsing the map with his garlic fingers.

"That's what he said," confirms Melody. "*Catch him if we can!*"

We both look at the map. The location The Falcon gave us is just an empty lot. There's no building there. Scammers will be scammers, I guess.

"Can we at least confirm that address?" I ask.

"Oh, it's confirmed," Melody says, tilting her head. "Cookie already wired the deposit."

Well, I guess we'll have to trust The Falcon will honor the hackers' code.

"By the way Michael, I just put your name in the bucket," Tiko says. "What are you gonna sing, jungle boy?" he asks.

I will have to think for a second.

Islands in the stream?

43

Honeymoon Suite

Melody and I just finished consummating the marriage, and she's now resting her face on my chest. I'm stroking her wavy hair. The freckles might leave a mark though.

"You just keep saying *yes* to anything?" I ask her.

"Yes."

I don't see her face, but I can feel her smile in my neck. Soothing air comes from the balcony, sending the white curtains dancing.

"There will be moments where you feel uncertain." She whispers. "Fear not. That's how great adventures begin."

I let that sink in.

"So tell me then, what exactly do you like about me? I mean, saying *no* appears to be kind of my default setting."

She laughs. "You've made progress, my dear adventurer. We're far from that dreadful day at *La Piscina*. Remember? You wouldn't put a toe in that water. But somehow, deep in there, you were still curious. And that day, curiosity was stronger than anything else."

She pulls her head up and kisses me.

"That's what I like about you," she lays out. "The fact that you still believe in magic. That makes you both naive and strong."

We both fall asleep.

44

The Falcon

"You've done that before?" I nervously ask Tiko, while Melody and I cover the exits. We both keep an eye on the entrance of the underground garage buried deep below the business district. Cyrus prays in the corner. I hope he has network down here.

Tiko wiggles the door handle of a Kia Optima, of all things.

Docking and disembarking in the port of Panama City was a piece of cake. Unfortunately, the Falcon instructions are pretty clear. We need to pick him up at that empty lot located just outside of the downtown core.

And we don't have a car. That is yet.

Renting one would take forever, plus, we don't have any IDs anyways. By the grace of God, Tiko is a former car thief.

"Ever heard of the KIA Boys?" he asks, as he finally manages to pop the car door. He then pulls out his phone and a USB cable he just bought aboard the cruise ships. Upsells again!

"The internet has plenty of videos from teenagers stealing KIA cars using a simple smartphone app, and a cable that hooks directly into the console. Triggering the engine to start with the push of a button."

Tiko was one of them.

From what I gathered, car thieves favor the *Kia Optima, Soul, Forte* and *Sportage* models produced between 2011 and 2018, because they have *the push to start* feature and the cable jack. Last year alone, roughly eighty thousand of these KIA models were stolen this way. And the car company has been rushing ever since to fix that flaw. Releasing updates and patches and whatnot.

"Get in!" Tiko whispers, as he starts the engine.

"Unbelievable," says Melody, jumping shotgun. "We got six hours left before boarding back on the Majestic. That should be plenty of time to catch the Falcon and go through the bank safety deposit box."

Tiko floors it, and the car emerges on the busy streets of Panama City. A grid we're both totally unfamiliar with.

Feels weird to be back into the real world after roughly a month off the map. Far at sea or deep in the jungle. Can't say that I like what I see. It's quite shocking actually. Too many billboards. Too many signs and logos everywhere. Only now do I notice that.

From the backseat, I follow the GPS on the console, telling Tiko which way to merge and where to turn at the last second. Like a good rally partner.

Panama City is quite extensive. Far from the mosquito infested ravine Roosevelt inherited after The French government forfeited the task to dig the first canal.

Investors buy here because they know that if somehow shit hits the fan, the US will swoop in. There's just too much at stake to lose control of the area. The canal alone generates five billion a year in revenue.

We drive by a Banana Republic store, how ironic. Ultimately, we reach the vacant lot, and the GPS lady finally shuts up. Tiko leaves the car running, just in case.

"Where is this Jackass?" Melody asks. "We're right on time."

We face the empty lot. Not far behind, white condo towers form the city limit. All designed as if they no longer speak to each other.

"Hold on, is that…?" Tiko says, pointing up at the sky.

"The goddamn Falcon," Melody replies with a smirk. "Right on cue."

Coming down real fast is a man wearing a wingsuit, red and

blue. He probably jumped off one of those condo towers.

"He's not gonna make it," mumbles Cyrus as The Falcon gets dangerously low without deploying.

The Falcon finally pops the parachute, grabs the handle and glides the rest of the way. "Start the car! Start the car!" he shouts still mid-air.

"It's rolling," Tiko says, amused.

The Falcon performs an elegant slide on the grass while applying the brakes to finally immobilize ten feet away from the KIA. Doors wide open.

"Quick, help me fold the *chute*!" The Falcon rushes.

"Nice to meet you," snarks Melody.

He looks at us over the frame of his foggy skydiver's glasses.

"Go, go, go, they're coming," he warns us as he jumps in the back of the car, holding the parachute in a ball.

"Who's coming?" shouts Tiko from the driver's seat. All spooked up.

The Falcon laughs.

"They can't catch us all," he says. "They just can't!"

Through the passenger windows, we can spot more flying squirrel men falling from the sky and aiming in our direction.

Tiko goes full throttle, following the directives The Falcon shouts from the hatch.

"What? You want me to drive back into the city?" Tiko asks, perplexed. "Are you nuts?"

"Yes, I'm gonna jump again. The police can't catch us all." The Falcon says, locked in. "There's too many of us. Authorities call us *The Empty Nesters*, because we jump from vacant condos brokers put on the MLS."

Interesting guy.

"So yeah, I'll try to sneak in another jump before lunch. Got the money?" presses The Falcon.

He hands Melody a manila envelope that she opens, dropping the documents on her lap as Tiko swerves between the narrow lanes of the financial district.

"You got two passports, a driver license for Micheal and a bus card for you. For street cred."

The Falcon grabs both passports from her hand and messes them up a little. Scratching the covers, and tapping the corners on the window frame before handing them back to us.

"You're a pro," says Melody. She throws him a roll of $50k.

"Here, on the curb. Pop the trunk," The Falcon says. "You're good, relax. The police have better things to do." He jumps from the trunk, his parachute still rolled up in a ball. "Oh, and nice car by the way."

And that was it for The Falcon.

"Where's the bank?" Tiko asks.

Melody browses the GPS. "It's two blocks away."

That's when we decided we could do the owner of the KIA a little favor. Because I'm pretty sure that by now, he wishes his ride would disappear for good. Even better, totaled. Entitling him to a full refund.

Therefore, we put a brick on the gas and aim the SUV at the canal.

A little pump and dump.

45

The Treasure Chest

Security guards in the lobby of the bank only glance for a millisecond at our American passports before handing them back to us. All this for that?

We then move onto the bank teller with the confidence of Mr. and Mrs. Smith. I pluck the silver necklace from under my shirt and lay it on the marble counter, unsure of what the process is supposed to be.

The teller grabs the key and inspects it for a second.

"Welcome back number 227."

Melody remains stoic. We're both pretending to be bored with the protocol yet inside, my heart is playing pong. Is that it? The day we finally dig up the Captain's treasure?

The bank teller pushes a button, and the gate buzzes open. We follow him down the marble hallway, passing many small rooms containing rows of safe deposit boxes. Shoes go tic tac. That's it, take us to the VIP section, brother. Take us to the big boys' locker room.

The teller stops in front of a vault door guarded by a tall armed man. Not local. Slavic looking. They both twist a key at the same time and don't say shit. Then the bank clerk punches a code on the numerical pad.

The vault opens.

"Take your time," the teller says. "Ring the bell when you're done, and Rodrigo will buzz you out. As always, thanks for doing business with us."

The vault door closes behind us.

"Should we have sex, now?" I ask Melody. She smiles, grabbing the necklace from my hand.

"Number 227, he said?" she mumbles, gliding the key top to bottom over the many rows of safe deposit boxes.

"Here," I tell her, before she twists the key inside to release the coffer. It's quite light for a treasure chest.

We drop the box on the center table.

Melody opens it.

Inside of the box, we find a simple paper document.

"THE FOUNTAIN CORPORATION"

It's a company title deed detailing the following ownership:

Tyler Cosgrove 50%
Bradley Smith 50%

Classification: Bio Tech

Melody puts a hand to cover her mouth. Still shocked, not knowing how to react.

"Look!"

Under the two-page document, there's a photograph.

One single picture.

It shows the aerial view of what looks like a *blue hole*. A geological formation you can find all over the Bahamas and the Yucatan Peninsula. It's a deep hole filled with fresh water. Usually the entry point connecting to a network of underwater caves.

"The Fountain," Melody whispers.

I flip the photo over and at the back, we can read:

COME FIND ME.
-Tyler

46

Geoguessing

Back on The Ocean Eyes, back on Cookie's menu. God bless her. Also, back under the protectorate of the Albino.

All swords united under one flag. The flag of an expedition about to venture deeper on the path of The Fountain.

Another clue on this island chain of events. Sailing together towards majestic conquests. And in due time, escaping tides shall reveal more signs along the way.

In the war room, the whole crew is assembled.

"So Tyler is alive and well?" the Albino asks, looking at the signed photograph of the blue hole.

"We believe so. And that safety deposit box was probably the only way Tyler could send Brad a message. Sooner or later, the Captain would have gone back."

The Albino grunts. "Wish he had thought of that before sending me to the snake pit."

I look at everyone around the table for a moment.

"On the day we killed the Captain" I begin. "When I was alone with him on the bluffs, he told me something, which at the time, sounded kinda odd. The blabbering of a drunk and exhausted man. Devoured by cancer and jealousy."

Nobody says anything.

"He told me *The Fountain, Tyler and the treasure. He told me that these things... they were all the same.*"

Everyone stares down at the corporation papers.

"What is this, then? Some medical utopia for billionaires?" asks the Albino.
Cookie flips through the document, but there's nothing else in there.

"So The Fountain is real, after all?" asks Cyrus.

"Oh, it's very real," Melody says. "And according to that piece of paper, we own fifty percent of it."

"Now what? Are we supposed to go look for this blue hole on a hunch? Locate this thing based on a single aerial photo?" the Albino asks.

Speaking of which.

"We have the technology on our side," I tell them, quickly deploying my laptop on the table. "We just need to run this picture against the satellite maps database until we have a decent match."

And in seconds of the data analyzing, a location is revealed. The software found a match on some small island off the coast of Belize. A quick online search produces a link to a luxury real estate website. That island was listed for sale recently. But not anymore. That link is dead.

Interesting.

"New captain, shall we?" Melody asks.

"Tiko, pull up the anchor!"

47

A Muddy Start

Trekking with scuba diving equipment in the jungle is not ideal. According to the satellite map, this blue hole is roughly two miles north of where we anchored The Ocean Eyes. Another mysterious island, yet this time we arrive with an invitation.

Cookie stayed back to keep an eye on the yacht, same thing for the shaman. We're done with the esoteric after all. The Fountain turns out to be backed by pure science.

Some billionaires venture into the field of life extension. Playing God in paradise.

The scuba fins strap keeps sliding off my shoulder. That oxygen tank alone is thirty pounds. No choice if we want to explore the secrets of the deep. The Albino brought a harpoon just in case.

"We got similar holes like this back in Tulum," Tiko explains, trekking behind me. "They are formed by fresh water carving its way through the porous rock and towards the ocean. Over the years, it created a vast underwater river system. Most of them are connected. Think of it as a sponge, in which you can swim from one bubble to the other."

"It's very dangerous though, experts only," Melody adds, turning around to face us. "That's why you guys are gonna play dead sticks today. Okay? The Albino and I will gently tow you two goofy floaters along."

"What do you mean?" I ask her.

"The mud," Tiko says. "This is some next level scuba shit."

"Sediments, to be exact," Melody says. "As we swim down the hole, mud and deposits will start to float around, obscuring everything. We gotta progress very slowly."

"And if one of you guys decides to panic and starts kicking around, we're all dead. Remember that," warns the Albino. "We won't be able to find our way back up."

That's horrible.

"There, an opening," points out the Albino, leading the pack.

Ahead, the thick jungle clears up and the giant freshwater hole reveals itself. A pristine blue. It's hard to picture the whole thing from the ground where we stand, and whether this hole is the right one. I guess we're about to find out.

"What is that?" Tiko asks pointing at the blue.

In the middle of the water, floats a yellow buoy.

"I guess that's the doorknob," Melody says. "Time to zip up. Time to lock in."

Once we've swam our way to the middle of the pond, we find a rope attached to the yellow buoy. The rope goes all the way down to the bottom where it's dark.

We don't have radio communications in the scuba gear so we rely on makeshift visual commands. The Albino looks pretty at ease in this underwater world, given his beluga size. Clipped to his back, Tiko looks like a small suckle fish tagging along for the ride.

They go first, pointing the harpoon while Melody is pulls on the leash connecting the two of us. I give her the universal okay sign, and we begin our descent.

And they were right, immediately the settled debris starts to float in all directions, bouncing off the light from our frontal lamps.

Attached to a tank full of air, never has my mind been so empty. Focused. The man in the mask. Obsessed with what could lie at the end of that rope.

What are we gonna tell Tyler? That we killed his best friend? That we came down here to claim our share of the loot?

The rope goes into a hook drilled into the rock at the bottom of the hole and starts to shoot off horizontally. This time sideways into a cavern. Our frontal lamps detail rows of stalactites we carefully try to avoid. I play the dead stick the best I can as Melody keeps dragging me along.

I'm looking at the depth gauge, and it says twelve meters. My ears tell me worse.

We've been gliding like this for a mile maybe. How long can we last? Then another hook, this time sending the rope back up along a rocky shaft. Not more than three meters wide. This is crazy. But at least we're going up towards the light.

Once we reach a depth of 10 meters, we can see the surface breaking up. Rays of green lights.

And then there's a ladder.

48

Code Red

Tiko is the first to crawl up the ladder. I follow closely to finally pop my head out of the water. Where the hell are we? Upon a first look, this place has been excavated. Carved like an old mine or a bunker. And above, green lights run on a wire all the way down a long tunnel.

We remove the scuba masks and turn around to sit on the concrete slab to take off the fins. That's when all of the lights turn red. Different ambiance, I gotta tell you. Followed by the sound of an alarm.

"You already rang the doorbell?" teases Melody and she quickly rolls onto the slabs to make way for the Albino. He pops out in a flash.

As we rush to unbuckle the equipment, heavy footsteps echo down the tunnel. And soon enough, we're surrounded by a bunch of white lab coats holding semi-automatic weapons. That's a cool look, I admit.

Meanwhile, the Albino clenches to the harpoon.

"Hands up!" shouts a tall man with surfer blond hair, while one of his acolytes shuts down the alarm.

We're back to green lights at least.

"Who the hell are you? And how did you find my lab?" asks the handsome blond man, quite shocked.

The albino drops the harpoon and shows his hands like the rest of us.

"I'm Tyler, by the way. Who's in charge?"

We all look at each other. Nobody speaks.

"Oh boy," says Tyler.

That's when I pull out the blue hole photograph pinned to the corporation papers which I kept sealed in a plastic bag under my scuba suit. Our precious invitation.

"Lower the guns, would you?" orders Tyler to the lab coats upon recognizing the aerial snapshot.

He moves forward and plucks the photo from my hand. He stares at it for a second. Then turns it over to inspect his own signature.

"That was before we built the runway," Tyler laughs. Well,

friends. Glad you guys at least found the backdoor."

He looks at the four of us standing there, fish out of water.

"Now where is Brad?"

49

Project 1 : Mind and Matter

"You built all of this in six months?" I ask Tyler, baffled at the scope of his operation, the length of the tunnel and the underground infrastructure it involves.

The five of us ride in a golf cart with Tyler at the helm, followed by lab coats driving a separate buggy.

The green lights tunnel leads to a much bigger room carved out of the bedrock. A giant lab. And inside, a dozen more white coats are busy running different machines and workstations. Most of the equipment looks medical to me.

"We didn't build anything," explains Tyler. "We just brought in the equipment. The island itself, I bought from the Belize government. It's a former British-Honduras radar outpost from the 60's. Complete with barracks, nuclear power generators and water filtration systems. What the realtor called a *turnkey*. Can you believe it?"

At the center of the lab, scientists are sliding someone into what looks like a glorified MRI machine. Some kind of giant tube. With fiber optic wires running in every direction. Feeding the other workstations.

On the wall, there's a drawn map of the island. I can see the blue hole, also the landing strip connected to a series of hangars. Some other small buildings line up in the jungle. And above the map, video monitors show a video feed of every area. There on camera four, it's the scuba ladder where we came from.

"The government was quite happy to sell me this rusty rock and look the other way," Tyler adds, as he puts the golf cart in reverse to park it next to a row of computer servers.

"Now tell me, what did Brad tell you guys exactly?" asks our host.

The Albino looks at me, then Melody.

"Brad told us that you ran away with the money," she says bluntly.

"And that you probably worked for the Feds," adds the Albino.

Tyler laughs, slaps his thigh.

"God damn, Brad. That's rich. He's never been able to trust anyone," Tyler shrugs, waving a hand over his head. "All I did was for *us*. See, I managed to save the money. Then I hid it from the Feds until I ended up here. Laying the cornerstone to begin the most important work of all."

"The Fountain," I whisper.

Melody sighs.

"He was getting very sick at the end," she recounts. "His cancer was spreading fast, and he felt like he was running out of time."

"He got delusional, jealous and greedy," I add. "That's when he tried to kill me."

Melody grabs my hands. Tyler gets a picture of what's going on.

"That's a damn shame," he says, looking down. "We could have fixed him here, you know? That's the whole point of The Fountain, isn't it?"

We all look at Tyler, waiting for him to continue with the tour, because for now, all of this is still rather confusing. My brain has gone electric.

"What is the goal here, Tyler?" I ask for the whole crew.

He takes a deep breath.

"That's the end game, my friends. What we couldn't find in nature, I've created. Carving the first path to eternal life."

We all step out of the cart and follow Tyler onto the lab floor.

The lab coats don't seem to mind us.

"Sounds a bit like science-fiction," challenges Tiko.

Tyler stops, turns to him, dead serious.

"Science, yes. Fiction, no," he replies.

Tyler runs a hand through his blond hair and as we move towards the center of the lab.

"I've assembled on this God forsaken rock, some of the leading scientists from the most controversial fields of medicine. Stem cells research, brain imagery, psychedelics. Most of their research is kinda *hush-hush* and controversial back in their home countries. These scientists were quite happy to score fresh funding, and a safe place to pursue their experiments uninterrupted."

He brings us around the central station. Inside the giant tube, someone is being scanned. Lots of light inside that pours out through the fiber optic.

"What you are looking at, is Project 1: *Mind & Matter.*"

"That's a lot of bleep bloop," remarks Tiko, looking at the control panel and the messy wires going in all directions.

Tyler looks at him, then to us. "You guys brought me an interesting specimen here! Can't wait to run you through the machine, my little friend."

"What is this machine doing?" Melody asks.

"This is still very early stage," Tyler explains. "But what we are trying to achieve in this lab, is to create a digital version of the brain. Some blueprints of individual minds."

"I've read about this," I quickly jump in. "Apparently scientists managed to map the entire brain of a fruit fly."

"Yes. And we're leaping fast. It's only a matter of time until we scale that up to a chinchilla, then a human."

The Albino looks puzzled. What's in your head, zombie?

"We don't need to scan the whole thing, you know," Tyler continues, as he taps on Tiko's forehead. "There is something special in there that makes *you*, you! We're trying to get to that essence."

Fascinating. We all stare at Tyler, mouths wide open. The scanner still runs, emitting intricate particles of light.

"And once we combine that brain image of yours, along with your DNA sequence, what we obtain is basically a digital copy of *you*."

We let that sink in.

"What are you gonna do with these *digital copies*?" the Albino asks.

"We're gonna shoot them into space!"

50

Project 2 : Echos of Humanity

The golf cart is rolls on the tarmac. A little sun feels great after we spent the last couple of hours underwater / underground.

I think we're all still trying to wrap our minds around what Tyler wants to achieve on this island.

A digital copy of ourselves. Shipped to the stars? And I thought Brad was eccentric.

At the end of the landing strip, another surprise awaits.

"Look at that!" Melody shouts.

Out there, a rocket is assembled in its upright position. Pointing up to the blue sky.

"It's rather small?" Tiko wonders.

"It's because we don't need to ship any flesh and bones,

remember? We're just shipping the blueprints. And whoever or *whatever* will discover our probes in the future, might be able to rebuild us."

Slow down, handsome devil.

It's true. Humans have been scattering DNA through space for a while now. It started with the Apollo missions and a small capsule left on the moon's surface. We also sent probes to Mars' moon Phobos, among others. And by "we", I mean, humanity, you know.

The novelty of Tyler's plan though, is also to ship digital fragments of our conscientiousness. This part I understand. *Mind and matter.*

The cart circles behind the launchpad, and on the other side of the rocket, I read "ECHO" labeled on the fuselage.

"Our first launch is scheduled for two weeks from now," Tyler explains, driving closer towards one of the open hangars.

"And where is this probe going?" Melody asks, totally geeking out about the plan. She's been flying drones and small planes for years. But this. This is the major league.

"This one is going straight to Alpha Centauri, the nearest star system," Tyler replies, with his chin up to the clouds.

"But that's light years away!" I tell him.

"4.36 light years away, to be exact," Tyler replies.

Everyone looks puzzled.

"First, you need to remove yourself from the equation, Micheal," he continues. "Your little lifespan doesn't mean anything on the scale of the cosmic calendar."

He has a point.

"Once we've successfully launched this probe, the rockets will keep going and going until someone or something finally catches us."

Tyler brings the cart inside of the open hangar. Inside, half a dozen engineers are bent over schematics. They look busy calculating trajectories and what seems to be fuel requirements.

There are two massive fuel tanks sitting in the back, with yellow piping running all the way to the launchpad.

"You guys deserve some refreshments, I believe," Tyler declares, stepping out of the buggy and motioning towards the lounge area.

Some couches and cold beer. We're back to earth.

Tyler mimics a rocket launch with a bottle.

"The location of our island is perfect to launch rockets into space. Since we're located near the equator, we benefit from maximum earth's rotation."

Tyler turns around towards the fuel tanks.

"For the first stage of propulsion, we use standard boosters filled with liquid fuel. This will provide escape velocity to clear earth's orbit."

Tyler pops the bottle cap and ditches the bottle.

"Then, the ion engines will take over for the rest of the journey. And before you say science-fiction again, my little man, we I have the technology. With the current state of this tech, the probe should reach Alpha Centauri within fortythousand years."

We all take a generous sip.

"We plan to launch new probes steadily every six months for as long as we can manage. Hence the name of the project. In forty thousand years, humanity might be long gone. But the universe will still hear our echo."

51

Stargazers

"And I thought Brad was intense," Melody says says, staring into the fire.

We managed to escape the time share presentation from Tyler and find a cozy spot to drink on the beach. Not exactly the chill utopia we were hoping to find.

"I wanna go home," Tiko says.

"We'll leave in the morning. I miss my girl," the Albino confirms.

The sky is clear, and the view of the universe above is infinite. Majestic.

"I mean, what's the point of living forever if you are stuck on this island? Let alone strapped to a rocket on its way to nowhere. With fingers crossed."

Tiko is right. Plus, he said it best before. On the day I met him back in Tulum.

The only way to cheat death is to live.

"Should we ask Tyler for our money back?" Melody jokes.

She slides closer on the log next to me, puts her head on my shoulder and a kiss on my neck. My treasure, I got it right here. I had to come all this way and fight all those battles to realize that one thing.

What's in the stars is in the fire.
You're never really far from whatever you desire.

Waves are the only thing crashing the silence.

Until we hear that awful thing again. The loud sound of the alarm. This time coming from the launch pad.

"What the hell," the Albino shouts, getting up in a hurry and trying to look over the bluffs.

Then the violent sound of an explosion, with electric flashes and fire rising up in the distance.

Oblivious to danger, we all start running towards the hangars. At the end of the tarmac, a silhouette waves a flamethrower. Shooting bursts of fire and gasoline all over the place.

Once the fuel tanks are set ablaze, the fire starts running along the pipes and towards the launch pad, forming a giant wall of flames. The silhouette grows darker by contrast.

"I would recognize that gait in a million..." the Albino whispers.

"Is that?" Melody asks, slowly covering her mouth.

Motherfucking Captain Brad.

I thought I killed you.

52

A Circle of Fire

Soon, the white coats and the golf carts rush to the scene. Rolling onto the tarmac only to be stopped by the intense heat coming from the brazier.

"Holy Roman Empire!" Tyler shouts in awe of the devastation. Still, he pleads to his crew to hold gunfire.

Pieces of burning blueprints snow down everywhere. The twisting metal of the blazing hangars echo sounds from hell as they finally collapse.

"Brad, please stop!" Tyler shouts to his former partner.

But it's too late. Everything is ruined. The rocket, the hangars. Everything burns. With the skies dark and orange from their friendship being nuked.

The captain keeps spraying flames all around him on the tarmac, producing an impenetrable circle of fire.

"If I can't have it, nobody will!" Brad screams, his image blurred by the emanating heat.

Next to me, Tiko is in shock. "How is it possible? How could he have survived that fall?" he whispers. "I saw him die."

We move closer to the circle of fire and only then, can we see how badly mangled the old Captain is. With half of his face scorched. His left arm rendered completely limp. The flame thrower is only squeezed between his shoulder and his chest. A pitiful scene. A wounded animal backed into a corner.

Brad finally sees me.

"And you! You!" he screams, pointing the nozzle at Melody and I, killing us with his one good eye, staring devil across a wall of flames.

"How did you find us?" Melody dares to ask.

The captain laughs. "You stole my goddamn ship, you stupid idiots!" he shouts back from behind the fire. "I've been tracking you for days."

Melody moves closer to me, clinging to my arm. Tyler now steps forward. Would someone put the Captain out of his misery already?

"It's not too late, Brad," Tyler attempts. "We can still fix you! That was the whole plan, remember? We fix you, then we fix the world."

"How can you fix what is gone?" Brad says with his head down. The circle of fire gets tighter.

For the first time, the broken man lowers the flame thrower. Lost in his thoughts for a hot minute. Devoured by the last train station regrets.

Tyler motions to his crew to stand back. Maybe Brad will come to reason? But the Captain doubles down on anger.

"Look at me," Brad mumbles, now hardly sobbing. "Look at me!" he shouts again. "You turned me into a monster!"

On the surface, maybe. We can all agree. The face and the arm, we did that. Yet inside, it's greed that did the rest. Jealousy and greed. That was the Captain's real cancer.

He has been searching the whole world, and still, he's gonna die with a question on his mind.

So close yet so far.

And now with one final look towards his former partner, and then Melody and the rest of the crew, Captain Brad finally backs away into the fire. The backpack detonates. Bright flames engulf the dark silhouette.

This time, he was not spared. But the Captain was free. At last.

53

To New Adventures

When the sun rises over the tarmac, there's nothing left. Except for a giant pile of fuming metal. Only dust of what could have been. That forever quest for something missing. Somewhere between science and fiction. Puzzle pieces now deep down underneath the rubble.

The white coats have been busy all night trying to contain the flames on the runway. They managed to save the labs and the barracks.

"We will rebuild," Tyler said. "We've got a waiting list full of rich people dying to live forever."

He says that, yet it sounds a bit mechanical. Like most of the stuff on this island. His heart is broken. Finding his best friend only to lose him again. This time for good.

They might rebuild, but we won't stick around to find out. All of us already made plans for the next chapter of our lives.

We're all packed and aboard the dinghy, jumping waves. The Fountain is fading away in our rear view.

Cookie and the Albino will sail together. They will take good care of The Ocean Eyes. Maybe they'll start a family on international waters? Raising little pirates.

They made a promise to circle around to drop Tiko and Cyrus back in Tulum. I've heard them discussing plans to start something of their own. Another small piece of paradise, better curated. This time, not owing anything to anyone.

As for Melody and me, we've decided to catch a plane from Belize to Bali, Indonesia. We figured it was best to put an ocean between us and the cartels. Apparently, there's a great surf wave out there coming from the left. And she says we already have friends waiting for us.

We did not ask Tyler for half of the money.

Just a couple of million, of course.

Enough to feed the monster.

THE END

This book was written at:

- Desa Potato Head in Bali
- Zyn Café in Canggu, Bali
- Dépanneur Café in Montreal
- Foil Gallery in Montreal
- Delray Beach, Florida

About the Author

Jeff Lee lives in Montreal, Canada, where he works in advertising, real estate, and television. **Songs of the Sirens** is his second novel. He believes there are many wonders we haven't seen yet.

9 781069 103512